THE SECRET OF BRIDD

To Kayla,
Enjoy the story!
M Smith
oct. 8/14

THE SECRET OF BRIDD

M. D. Millar

Illustrations by Floyd Ryan Yamyamin

authorHOUSE®

AuthorHouse™ LLC
1663 Liberty Drive
Bloomington, IN 47403
www.authorhouse.com
Phone: 1-800-839-8640

Published by AuthorHouse   07/16/2013

ISBN: 978-1-4817-7741-4 (sc)
ISBN: 978-1-4817-7740-7 (e)

Library of Congress Control Number: 2013912676

Any people depicted in stock imagery provided by Thinkstock are models, and such images are being used for illustrative purposes only.
Certain stock imagery © Thinkstock.

This book is printed on acid-free paper.

Because of the dynamic nature of the Internet, any web addresses or links contained in this book may have changed since publication and may no longer be valid. The views expressed in this work are solely those of the author and do not necessarily reflect the views of the publisher, and the publisher hereby disclaims any responsibility for them.

To my son, Robert Patrick, for being the inspiration behind the story and to my husband, Costin, who supported me during this wonderful endeavor.

CONTENTS

The tall, white haired man was standing in front of the windows looking at the cold rain pouring down over the men hurrying about their duties down in the yard. They were wrapped in heavy cloaks that were meant to keep them dry but the wind was fluttering them around. They were trying to wipe their wet faces with the backs of their hands only to get them wetter. Horses were being saddled or harnessed to large wagons. Some of the men looked worried but went on with the preparations anyway. Some were hugging their children and wives, while some were just standing there in the rain, looking at the palace like saying good bye to it.

The old man turned away from the commotion in the yard and stopped in front of the portrait of a beautiful woman. She was wearing dark burgundy robes and the delicate tiara on her head was holding back her beautiful chestnut brown hair. She had a delicate necklace around her neck. The pendant in the shape of a bird with spread wings was hanging off a simple silver chain. A few curls left free on each side of her smiling face made her look very young and the man looked at her fondly. A wide, yet delicate smile showed the pearls of her teeth and the cherry red lips.

The man turned his face away briefly to look again at the rain hitting mercilessly the windows and talked to the woman in the picture in a sad voice.

"Today is the day, my dearest, today we will stop being . . . *us*. I don't know if I will meet you up there amongst the spirits of our Ancestors once all of this is over. But we have to do it, or else . . ." He stopped, his voice breaking, and looked at her again.

". . . We are the only ones who can stop . . . *him*. We have the *power* to stop him and we have to do it to save everybody from his tyranny. Good bye, my love, watch over us from above and help us set everything right."

He turned around and with a sad smile grabbed his helmet and sword lying on the chair beside him and headed toward the doors. He wrapped his body in the dark cloak covering the light armour decorated with the coat of arms of the kingdom. Under it, the white silk shirt embroidered around the neck and cuffs was neatly tucked in the soft leather pants. The knee high boots were shiny and the spurs made a soft jingling sound when he walked.

He stopped and looked at the portrait one last time and thought of his children. They had a good life, without wars or worries, but now, that was about to change. He had a long and prosperous life and was not sad to see it end sooner than he would have liked. Next year he would have turned 100 and he would have had many more years ahead. But his earthly life coming to an end only meant that he would join the Ancestors and hopefully be with his wife again.

Lost in thought, he turned when the doors opened behind him to see a young man, looking just like the woman in the portrait, entering and bowing his head with respect. He looked at the man and whispered.

"We are ready, Father, everybody is waiting for you." The young man looked at the portrait on the opposite wall and smiled. It looked like the woman smiled back at him and he looked surprised and a little scared.

"She knows, my son, she knows what we have to do today and she will look after us when we will need it, like she always did," the older man answered and put his arm around his shoulders.

"I'm ready too," he said softly, opening the doors. "May the Ancestors be with us!"

CHAPTER 1

Story Time

Once upon a time, a long, long time ago, there lived a wise King who ruled over land as far as he could see. The people living under his rule had never known war or hardship; they have been all living peaceful and prosperous lives, along with all living creatures around them. The King had many subjects—as many as the grass blades in the fields and the leaves in the trees. His name was Lade-Gleal and he had been ruling over his people for as long as anyone could remember. King Lade was a kind and fair ruler and because of that everybody called him Father Lade.

The people in Father Lade's kingdom liked open spaces where they could see the sky and the mountains and the forests. They lived on the open, rainy plains of the South or in the depths of the dark forests of the West, on top of the tall mountains of the East, in warm, damp marshes alongside the big rivers of the Midlands or in the cold, icy lands of the North.

The King and his family lived in their Ancestors' palace, in the city of Bridd. The palace was the oldest building in the city and although nobody remembered when it was built, its walls showed little signs of aging. The stone steps at the front were still shiny and the marble rails looked as if time did not touch them. Tall arched windows were giving the facade a distinguished majesty. The flags showing the kingdom's coat of arms and the county banners were fluttering in the breeze on top of the towers.

Inside, the rooms were bright and the tall windows were letting the sunlight filter through, warming up the gray stone walls. The throne room had its walls draped in velvety green curtains and rows of chairs lined the walls. While it was the largest room in the palace and was always prepared for all kinds of ceremonies, lately it was only used for the celebrations of the Day of the Kingdom. The room was deserted most of the time and rarely anybody would be in there. It served now as a passing room that would take people to the large Meeting Hall where family and guests were spending most of the time. The bedrooms and guest rooms were on the second floor of the palace and they offered an unobstructed view of the city or of the gardens.

The palace was surrounded by houses spread around, looking like smaller versions of the King's home. The wide, neatly kept streets converging at the palace, made the city look like a gigantic web. Surrounded by small peaked fences or tall hedges, they let the passersby enjoy the wide porches and well kept gardens. The city of Bridd was renowned for its beautiful, luxurious gardens and visitors from all over the land would come to see them and enjoy their colours.

People from all corners of the kingdom were coming to the City of Bridd all year long to bring their offers to their King and to enjoy the beauty of the palace gardens and its surroundings. In spring, gentle crocuses and snow drops were lining the path to the palace, competing with a symphony of purple and brown irises and golden daffodils. In summer, lavish vines were covering the tall walls of the palace and superb rose shrubs were greeting guests in a mélange of colours. Fall was bringing shades of brown and orange on its large trees and intricately cut hedges. Snowy winters turned the palace and its surroundings into a winter wonderland where people would meet on the frozen lake or under the warmed gazebos for hot drinks.

Father Lade and his Queen liked visitors and people from all over the kingdom would come to the city just to catch a glimpse of him in the gardens or to bring him a small token of their love and respect. The palace was always full of guests and food and drinks could be found in abundance for everyone to enjoy. Kings and rulers were coming over for spring celebrations or for the Harvest Festival. Tournaments were held every summer and celebrations of all sorts kept the kitchens and wine cellars busy.

There was one thing though, that all guests asked about and nobody could give an answer to: what the big rocks surrounding the kingdom at its borders were. The wind and rain have smoothed them and now they looked like tall, quiet sentries watching the borders of the Bridd land. Nobody knew why they were there and some would swear their number had grown in the past years.

Today on a day like any other, the King, his family and a few of their closest friends were having the morning meal in the dining room. The King was chatting softly with his First Councillor as the food was being brought in from the kitchens. His three sons with a few of their friends were laughing loudly at the other end of the table, while his younger daughter and her friends were whispering at one another, throwing quick looks at the young men at the other end. Llewella, his eldest daughter, was picking at her food, lost in thought, not listening to what they were saying. The King stopped talking and looked around the room, smiling fondly and thinking of his beloved wife. If she could see them now, how happy they all were, without a worry in the world.

The door to the dining room opened quietly and suddenly everybody stopped talking, looking inquisitively at the guard that entered the room. The man stopped in the doorway and waited for the King's permission to speak. Instead of asking him to come closer, the Councillor stood up and walked to him. The guard whispered something in his ear, then turned and left as quietly as he came. The King looked at his friend, as he noticed the worry on his face.

"What happened, Master Brohan? What did the guard want?" he asked and everybody looked at him anxiously.

"The scouts are back, My Lord, and they bring news from the borders. They are waiting in the War Room. As soon as we are finished, they would like to talk to you."

Everybody noticed the worry in the Councillor's voice but did not know what to make of it. The King stood up pushing his plate away leaving his meal barely touched, prompting everybody to stand up in respect.

"I'm done, you finish your meal," he told his companions. "I'll go talk to them now so they can go and rest. Master Brohan, would you come with me?" He smiled at everybody as to tell them everything was all right and left the room.

CHAPTER 2

Worrisome News

As the King was growing older, he was feeling lonelier every day. His Queen had fallen ill five years before and died soon after and he has been all alone in the palace ever since. Lately, the guests, who once were filling the hallways and large gardens, were coming in more and more seldom and even then, only for a short time. The food he once found so enjoyable seemed now tasteless and the wines had no flavour anymore.

In the past few weeks, there was something that worried the King even more: word of a cruel Emperor who was quickly moving closer to their borders, conquering lands and peoples in his way. The Emperor wanted all living things to bow to him or be destroyed. Some were saying his heart was made of stone and ice. Just a few days ago, the King's scouts brought news of him getting closer and closer to the Kingdom. "Any day now he would be at the borders, threatening to cross them and take over our cities and lands," sounded the news.

But King Lade was not worried for him or his family and he was not worried for his subjects either. His land was protected. He knew no one could come and take it away. He knew that anyone with ill thoughts would be stopped. The *Sentries* would stop anyone who would want to conquer the country, from crossing into the kingdom.

The scouts that have returned last evening brought worrisome news. From afar, they looked at the Emperor's army camp: it was immense. The tents that sheltered the soldiers spread over the entire field at the borders and at night the camp fires and torches looked like a myriad of fireflies. The cannons surrounded the camp and wagons carrying supplies were parked on the west and east sides guarded by armored soldiers. They had gotten closer at night, trying to listen in, maybe the soldiers would give away secrets, but they did not know anything about their master's intentions.

They had met with their neighbours and talked about making alliances, but everybody was too terrified at the thought of going to war and they were all thinking of surrendering without a fight. No one wanted to endanger the lives of their people and there was nothing to do about that. Myrdall, his Councillor's son was due to come back and bring more news about their enemy and he could hardly wait for him to return. Maybe he did manage to make some alliances with other kingdoms farther away and that should give them some time to prepare for the inevitable. If Myrdall was unsuccessful too, then their last hope was an old book and its contents that would tell them what to do in case of danger.

Many years ago, upon his coronation, his father told him that the kingdom was protected from invaders. He should not worry about anybody trying to enslave them. He did not tell him why that was—just that everything was written in the *Book of Wisdom* which was kept in the book storage down in the dungeons of the castle. Should the kingdom ever be threatened, he would only have to find the book, read it and he will know what to do.

The King's father and grandfather and their fathers before, never needed to read the book, as the land had never been threatened before. He would be the first one in a very long time to have to find it. What the book was about, no one alive knew. He will soon have to go down to the dungeons and find the book himself. Nobody else was allowed to see it—or read it—but the King himself: that was the law.

One of these days I will have to go and find the book, the King thought. Come to think of it, he has never been in the dungeons of the castle before. Why the Book of Wisdom was kept there and not in the Royal library was a mystery to him. The last time anybody went down there, was when his father had to take down a pair of wooden boxes. No one knew what those chests were for or what was inside them. His father never talked about them once they were locked down there and nobody ever asked. *One of these days*, the King said to himself, *one of these days . . .*

Day after day passed and the King almost forgot about the book. Today, the King was eating by himself, as his sons were visiting their cousins in the nearby city of Ribbel and they were not due back for another hour or so. The girls were having lunch in the gardens and his old friend, Brohan, the First Councillor, was busy with some papers and could not join him. As he was just finishing the meal, the noise of commotion down in the yard made him stop and look toward the window. He put down his napkin and moved toward it. In the courtyard, a young soldier was shouting something to the Chief of the Guards while pointing out west. The Chief turned to where the man was pointing and the King followed him. From the height of his room, he could see a small dot that was closing in fast. And as it was approaching the castle and was getting bigger, he could see the shadow of a rider appearing.

A knock on the door made the King turn to see who it was. Through the opening door, his first Councillor looked at him asking for permission to come in. Not moving away from the window, the King gestured to the man to come closer and pointing outside, asked.

"What is all the commotion about? Who is the rider coming in such a hurry?"

The Councillor moved closer to the window and not looking at his King, spoke slowly.

"It is my son, Your Highness, he is bringing news about the Emperor." He stopped, not knowing if he should continue. The King looked at him as if not understanding what he was talking about. Suddenly he remembered. *The Emperor, yes, he was moving closer to their land and he had to go find that book. He had forgotten all about it.*

"Master Brohan, have your son rest. Tell the cook to bring him something to eat and drink and then bring him to my chambers. I have something I must do now. Go and look after your son and we will talk later. I shall not be long."

Myrdall was restlessly pacing around the room. Gleal, the King's oldest son and heir, had joined them and was lost in thought, looking out the window when the King entered the room. He looked worried, but as soon as he saw them gathered there, he lightened up and invited everybody to sit. Then, he looked at the young scout inquisitively.

"My Lord," the Councillor started as the customs required, "bad news is what my son brings." He turned toward his son and nodded, encouraging him to talk.

"My King," started the young man standing up and bowing with respect, "the Emperor is almost upon our borders. His army is so large I could not see its end. If we have to go to battle we would be outnumbered one to five. He has cannons pulled by big horses and his soldiers are covered in armour from head to toe. We cannot defeat them by ourselves. We need help and I am afraid nobody wants to make an alliance against him." He stopped not knowing what else to say, turning to his father for help. Their eyes were now on the King who took his time to answer.

"We will not go to war, my friend," the King started, looking at them. "At least, not yet," he added quietly, raising his hand seeing his son was about to stand up in protest. "First we need to see what the Emperor wants," he continued, staring at him, "so I will send a party to meet with him and tell him to turn his army around and leave. We will show him that we *will* defend ourselves if we need to, but we would rather have him leave and let us be." He only paused as if he wanted to catch his breath and continued.

"Myrdall, I want you and my son Rehon to choose half a dozen men to accompany you to meet the Emperor and take my message to him. I will write to him asking him to leave and that we do not want to fight him. You will have to take the letter to him right away. As soon as you have his answer, hurry back. Your father and I have important matters to talk about. While you are gone, we will get ourselves ready for whatever faith throws at us."

He turned toward his eldest son who was now standing in expectation and ended. "Gleal, help Myrdall get ready for his trip. I will meet with the two of you in the War Room when I have the letter."

He turned to the Councillor and showed him to his private study. The young men understood they were dismissed and headed for the door. The King turned quickly as they were just leaving the room and called.

"You'll leave in the morning, at sunrise. Safe travels, Myrdall. May the Ancestors be with you!" The young man bowed and closed the door behind him and Gleal.

CHAPTER 3

The Book of Wisdom

It was late at night, but the King could not sleep. The secret revealed by the *Book of Wisdom* was too much to handle, even for him. The voice of his forefathers' Spirit was still ringing in his ears. The letters in the book were still burning his eyes.

"No one can know about this, King Lade-Gleal, not yet," the voice had told him. "Should anybody find out about what protects you before you make the necessary preparations, you will be at the mercy of the Emperor who will take over the land and enslave you and your people, without a chance to defend yourselves."

"There has to be another way," he had cried. "I cannot let the Emperor take our Ancestors' land without defending it."

"There is another way," the voice said, "but that means your lives will be changed forever. What you have now, will all be gone and you will not remember anything of the life you are living now. Is that what you want for you and your people?" The words were still reverberating in his ears. *Your life will be changed forever . . .*

As soon as the Councillor left the room to get his son ready for the meeting, the King opened a door hidden by big curtains and started walking down a narrow staircase. The only light was coming from tiny fat lamps fastened to the rock walls and the King was carefully feeling each step as he was going down. After a strenuous walk he finally reached the bottom. Grabbing the torch waiting on the wall he lit it from one of the lamps.

Now he could see the entire room: it was large and looked empty, with walls covered in cobs and lichen. The absence of windows made the space look eerie and gave the man chills down his spine. He turned around looking for a door. A couple of old-looking wooden boxes were stacked in one of the corners and for a moment he thought that he had seen them before. He wiped his sweaty forehead and, as he turned to his left, saw it.

He took a deep breath and moved forward to the only other door in the room. He struggled a little with it as he tried to open it, but it finally gave way and it uncovered another room, this one much smaller, only a passage. He entered and as he turned to his right, a narrow wooden door came into view. *This must be the entrance to the storage room*, he thought and then he stopped suddenly. *What if the book is not here anymore? What if it has been destroyed by the passage of time? What should he do then?* He reached forward to the brass handle that looked surprisingly shiny and new and pressed it.

The door sprang open as if its hinges had been just oiled and the King found himself in front of an enormous room whose walls were covered by shelves going all the way up the ceiling. The shelves were filled with books and brownish rolls of parchment. As he entered the room, torches on the walls suddenly lit up. Surprised, the King stepped back covering his face from the bright light.

Once his eyes got used to it, he tried to remember where the Book was. His father had told him about it, but that was a long time ago and he could not remember anything right now. He took a slow look around hoping that something would trigger the memory. As he brushed the shelves with his eyes, he noticed the absence of dust and cob webs. It all looked as somebody was looking after this place, dusting it and making sure everything was in its proper place. It looked strange, as he knew for a fact that nobody else had come down here in a very long time. As he was thinking about how strange this place looked like, he noticed a large book with golden spine and covers sitting closed on a small table in one of the corners of the room.

He moved closer and he knew right away that the golden book was the one he was looking for. It was lying there, just like somebody had retrieved it for him and placed it on the table. He put the torch out, placing it down by the wall and tried to lift it off the table.

I will take it with me and read it in my chambers, he thought. But the book wouldn't move. He tried one more time to lift it, again without success. *It must be fastened to the table, then,* the King said to himself and felt underneath it with his fingers to see what held the book in place. But nothing was there. Puzzled, the King went around the table, looking for some sort of a lock, but could not see anything. As he looked around to find something to help him pry it off the table, he heard a voice talking to him.

"You cannot take the Book out of this room, it is only meant to be read here, by the King only. Should anybody else read it, the protective spell over the kingdom would be broken."

The King turned around to see where the voice was coming from but could not see anyone. "Who is that talking?" he shouted while turning in place. "Who's there? Show yourself!" he shouted again reaching for the torch to use it maybe to defend himself and turning around he suddenly stopped in front of a large painting. He recognised in it one of his forefathers, but he could not remember his name.

"Are you the one talking?" he asked hesitating and moved closer as he was thinking about how strange it was to talk to a portrait in a picture. The figure in the picture did not move though, but the voice continued. "I have been living here for a long time. I am a spirit of the Ancestors and I have been looking after you and your people. You cannot see me, you can only hear me. If you are here now, then you must be looking for the Book of Wisdom."

Silence filled the room and the King tried to understand what he had just heard. *A spirit protecting them? Did they know the kingdom was in danger? How did they know that?* As soon as he thought of it, the voice went on again.

"All alive and departed souls in the kingdom are linked, my king. The spirit of each and every living soul in this land is linked to the spirits of the departed ones. All that happens is known by us and when help is needed we find out about it. You now need help to protect the land and when you came down here, when you opened that door, you connected with us. When you set foot inside this room, you made the link between your world and the world of the departed ones."

The voice stopped once more and the King looked around for proof that he was not imagining it all. There was nothing in the room that seemed to be the "voice". Not sure why, he looked at the book and explained.

"There is danger coming. An Emperor has been conquering lands and enslaved peoples and is now heading our way. I remembered my father's words and came down here to look for the *Book of Wisdom*. I need to find out how to protect us and I need the book." He stopped, not knowing what else to say.

"The Book cannot leave this room. The secret in its pages is to be kept here. No one can know about it. As soon as a stranger finds out about it, the spell will break and your land will be unprotected in the face of danger."

The King looked at the book again and then up at the portrait.

"I need to take it to my chambers. I need to know what to do and I cannot be gone for too long, or my people will come looking for me."

"THE BOOK CANNOT LEAVE THIS ROOM!" the voice boomed again. "You need to read it here, there is no other way." As the voice finished, a small chair appeared beside the table where the book was resting.

"What you need to know is here," the voice continued as the Book suddenly opened and the pages started to shuffle. As sudden as they started, that sudden they stopped and the King saw that the page the Book was opened at started with "Should our land ever be in danger . . ."

Sitting down in the small chair, he followed the letters with his eyes, not able to stop. *Should our land ever be in danger again, one should try not to engage in battle.* The word "not" was highlighted and he wondered why. *The Sentries at the borders will keep the enemy from crossing over, like they did eons ago. No one with ill thoughts can cross over or they will turn to stone as soon as they set foot on our land.*

Everyone will be turned to stone? thought the King. *All those rocks at the borders, the ones that people have been talking about—are they enemies who tried to come and harm us? What else was there to know?*

The King has to do everything in his powers to prevent war, the Book went on. *Only after everything has been tried, and negotiations have failed, then and only then, the King will raise the army. Should the King have to start preparations to go to war, he can only confide in his First Councillor and his heir. No one else can know about the secret spell that protects the land and people of the Bird Kingdom, until everybody is ready to understand the danger.*

"The Bird Kingdom? What is the Bird kingdom?" the King found himself asking aloud.

"The Bird people," the voice spoke again, "is the name of your Ancestors. They settled here after they left their native lands, a very long time ago. Nobody remembers this because it happened so long ago no one is alive today to tell the story. Even the legends have died with those who knew about it."

"All knowledge about what the kingdom once was has died with the last descendant of King Bird, long ago. The last King Bird had no children of his own and some members of his family—on his wife's side—have left these lands long ago. Nobody alive knows where they are now or what has become of them. Should they ever return, they would be the rightful heirs to rule the land."

Silence fell in the room once again, as the King tried to understand what the Spirit had just told him. *If the descendants of King Bird would return, they would have the right to rule? All this time he has believed that he and his son were the descendants of the First Peoples who lived on these lands. He thought that, when it would be his time to retire, his son Gleal would inherit the throne, as he inherited it from his father.*

Time seemed to stand still as he tried to figure out what to do. He could not take the book with him, but he had to return to the chambers, Myrdall should be ready to tell him what he found out about the Emperor. As if reading his mind, the voice spoke again.

"You must go back to your chambers, your son has been looking for you. Come back soon. You need to finish reading the book before the Emperor arrives at the borders."

The King stood up and just as sudden as it appeared, the small chair disappeared and the book closed. The lights went off and the King reached for the torch which lit immediately. He grabbed it and headed back up going through the door that closed behind him silently. Up in his chambers, his son and his guests were waiting.

CHAPTER 4

Emissaries

It was finally morning and Myrdall was ready to leave. The men were all waiting for the letter. The First Councillor was sitting in the big chair by the window, looking at his King pacing around the room gesturing and talking excitedly. He was listening to him talking but his mind was wandering, trying to find answers to the one question: what was this *book* he was talking about? He does remember his father talking about the *Book of Wisdom*, but nobody thought it actually existed. Everybody thought it was some legend that people liked to talk about, a story for children to hear on stormy winter nights.

"So, I have to go back and read the rest, to find out what we need to do if the Emperor does not turn back," he heard the King's voice in the distance. "The Spirit said there is another way to fight him, but that it would change our lives forever." The King stopped right in front of him and asked. "Can you take care of the council while I go back to the library to finish? You are the only one I can trust, aside from my son Gleal. And no one else can know about it." The Councillor nodded and finally spoke.

"My Lord, what is this Book you are telling me about? What is this spell? Nobody has heard about any *Sentries*. The big rocks at the borders—are they all enemies?"

The King looked at him in disbelief. "Do you think I have dreamt this last night or that I am losing my mind as I am growing older? For many years I thought it was just a legend, too, until I saw it and read it. I cannot bring it up here and I am not sure if you would be allowed to see it should you come down with me, but everything is as real as you and me." He stopped and looked worried at his old friend. "This is not the time to argue about this, my old friend, we need to get ready. Our army is not prepared for this, but I know our people would give their lives to protect the land we have been living on for so many generations. Let's find out what protected our country until now and how we can keep it the same." He looked out the window and sighed. Then he turned to his friend again and handed him the letter.

"Have my son and Myrdall take this to . . . *him* and when he returns, we will know what to do. I must go back down and finish reading. The council should have gathered by now, use your wisdom to tell them that we have to prevent war at all costs. Help me, my friend, just like you have always done." With a sad smile on his face, he left the room to go back to the book.

A new day was starting and Gleal was sitting alone in the throne room, away from the murmurs of the hallways and kitchens, looking at the forest far behind the palace.

The young prince loved autumn and on a normal day he would be out in the gardens enjoying the changing colours and remembering his mother. But today he was lost in thought, not looking at anything in particular—his eyes were just wondering around the deserted garden, over the leafless hedges and empty flower beds. He was listening to the rain rapping on the windows. Some time ago, he would have enjoyed listening to the rain playing its rhythmic tunes on the palace windows and walls, but today he found the rain to be mean and cold.

On a day like this he would be out hunting or target practicing or fencing with his younger brothers and his friends. But today he was worried and hoped that Myrdall and his younger brother would bring good news upon their return. He was not sure what kind of good news he expected, but he hoped that the Emperor would turn around or head towards other lands to conquer or maybe even go back to his lands. Of course it was not fair to think like that, but the thought of them going to war was something nobody was comfortable with. They did not have to go to war in a very long time, in fact, as far as he knew *nobody* had ever threatened their land in their life time, or his grandfather's. Their army was ready for parade days, for tournaments, but not for real battle.

News of the Emperor getting closer and closer to their land had everybody worried. Deep in thought, he did not notice someone coming in. He turned suddenly at the noise of the tall doors closing and raised his eyes to see his younger brother, Whock coming in. He was wearing his uniform and had his ceremonial dagger on the belt. In his left hand he was holding a small silver shield and in his right, his feathered helmet was gleaning in the light of the torches. His bushy eyebrows shadowed his bright, blue eyes. Worry covered his face too and as he moved closer, Whock looked at his brother inquisitively. But why was he dressed like that, Gleal wondered? He shook his head to make the bad thoughts go away and looked at his younger brother smiling.

"First Chancellor told me Myrdall just returned from a scout's mission and is getting ready to go back to meet . . . *him*," Whock started not letting his eyes off his brother. "Is it true the Emperor is getting near?"

Just then, Rehon entered the room followed by his friend, Myrdall.

"You heard right, my brother," he called as if he had heard him asking the question. Rehon was Gleal's younger brother and good friends with Myrdall. He was one year older than Whock, but the two looked like they were twin brothers.

"But I will let him tell you all about it," he continued. The two young men shook hands with Myrdall as he looked at them. "The Emperor is closing up on our borders. He is less than a week away and no one can stand up to him. His army is too strong for anybody who is trying to stop him." He paused for a moment and then looked at Whock.

"The King is sending us to meet the Emperor. We are leaving as soon as the horses are ready . . ." He paused and as his friend looked at him intrigued, continued ". . . to take *a letter* to him."

Gleal, who had been in that meeting and had heard the reasons why their father would not go to battle, looked down, then out the large windows. The wind was now blowing the rain drops against the glass and the sound resembled the rapping of arrows on practice targets.

"Father is preparing a message to send to the Emperor, Whock. He has asked the council to gather in the War Room and he is sending a party to him to tell him to turn around and leave us be." He sighed as he looked at his friends and continued.

"He does not want to fight the Emperor. He hopes to persuade him to turn around without having to engage him in battle."

Silence filled the room and the young men looked at each other in disbelief. *The King did not want to fight? Why? Does he really think the Emperor will just turn around and leave?*

"Why does Father think he can persuade the Emperor to turn around and leave? Is there something he knows that he is not telling us?" asked Whock while everybody looked at Gleal for an answer.

Gleal did not know what to say. Just as he was about to tell them that, the door opened and the First Councillor entered the room. The men bowed their heads with respect and Whock rushed to him.

"Master Brohan, we need to raise the army," cried Whock. "We need to fight for our land," the young man continued grabbing the Councillor by his arm. The Councillor looked at him and smiled. Then he turned to Gleal and explained.

"I know what you think, My Lord. That your Father is getting too old for this and that he should let you handle it. Trust your Father, Prince Gleal, our King will lead us on the right path, as he always did." He then turned to Rehon and handed him the letter.

"You take care of this, my prince, the King has put all hope in you two delivering it as soon as possible. Ride as fast as you can and come back soon with news. Ride swiftly, son," he wished to the two young men, "we look forward for your safe return." With a short bow he headed for the door.

The young men followed him as he left the room. Gleal and Whock, who stayed behind, looked at each other in disbelief.

"There is nothing you can do for now, brother," said Gleal. "Let's wait until Myrdall and Rehon are back. Father will then have to decide what to do next."

CHAPTER 5

Uncertainties

As soon as the emissaries left and the King went back to the dungeons, the Councillor headed for the War Room. The room was named the *war* room, but it had never been used to make battle plans, as for as long as he remembered there had been no wars on their land. Instead, the council would meet to discuss matters of land property, inheritance and passing new laws. The room was long and in the middle there was a beautiful wooden table, with carved legs that showed people working the land, gathering crops or other images inspired from their daily lives. The rectangular table was surrounded by tall chairs covered in brown leather. The table and chairs have been in the room forever too, nobody remembers it being different. The narrow windows let the grey light in, sifting it through the stained glass that pictured past kings. Today it looked as if the portraits were listening in, too.

The walls were draped in heavy curtains with scenes from battles that must have taken place long ago and that nobody remembered. The people in the scenes were tall and slim, and if you looked closer they did not look anything like the people living today in Bridd. Maybe it was the way they were dressed or the way their long wavy hair was fluttering in the wind . . .

The council members were all there, some discussing loudly and heated, others watching them and supporting one party or another. When Master Brohan entered the room they all fell silent and looked at him.

"His Majesty will join us later. He has asked me to come and tell you the news. My son, Myrdall, his majesty's younger son, Rehon and a party of six men are on their way to meet with the Emperor. They carry a message from our King, asking him to turn back. Our King does not want to fight him." Murmurs of disagreement started to rise in the room and he stopped them by putting up his hand.

"*Not yet*! My master told me we need to try and prevent war at all costs. FOR NOW!" he cried, as some were standing up in protest. "Should the Emperor refuse to leave, *then* we will go to battle. But now we need to wait for the emissaries to come back. Soon we will know what our fate is." He paused and before any of them could say anything, he dismissed them with a friendly smile.

"My friends, we need to trust our King. He will not let us down." Everybody nodded in agreement and started to head for the exit.

A few of them, though, stayed behind and approached the head of the council. They were all worried about the King's decision. They all hoped that their friend could give them some reason as to why the King was trying to avoid going to battle. They themselves hoped there would be no need to go to war, as they all knew they were not ready. But if they had to, they will defend their land—there was no question about it.

"Master Brohan," the Chief of the Guards started, "where is our King? Shouldn't he be here with us to tell us what needs to be done?" The others murmured in agreement and looked at Brohan.

"The King will join us as soon as he can. Right now he is finding out more about the Emperor and how we can defeat him." The men looked at each other surprised and a little offended by the answer. The Councillor sensed their disappointment and continued.

"There is something he needs to . . . consult," he hesitated, trying not to give up the real reason why the King was not with them. "When he is finished, he will join us and will share with us everything we need to know. Until then, we better go and look after our families and houses and get ready." They all nodded in agreement and silently headed for the doors.

As soon as everybody was gone, the Councillor sat down and put his head in his hands. He was glad the King was confiding in him, but he also felt the responsibility of keeping the secret too heavy on his shoulders. He did not know what the King will find in the Book and how much he will decide to share with everybody.

He understood that the "secret" had to be kept for now and he did not know what will happen when the others will find out.

He stood up and headed for the Meeting Hall just as Gleal appeared in the doorway. They looked at each other and smiled.

"Master," Gleal started, "I cannot find my father. Do you know where he is? I need to talk to him about his plans." Brohan looked at him and then away. He could not tell him anything, not yet anyway. He had promised to keep it between him and the King until he found out what the Book said.

"Your father had to meet with somebody and as soon as he is done, he will send for us." He stopped and looked him in the eye. "You need to trust your father's judgement, Gleal, he wants what is best for us. When he is ready to talk to us, he will."

The Councillor stopped talking and started moving toward the doors. Gleal moved closer to him and went on.

"Master, I know that he wants what is best for us. I am worried about going to war and I wish he would trust me as he does you. I am his heir and I need to know what to do should anything happen to him." He hesitated, ". . . or to you. My brothers and sisters, and everybody else, look up to me and I do not want to let anybody down. I want to walk in my father's footsteps but I feel he is keeping me away and I do not understand why. I do not want to disappoint him."

"You do not disappoint me, my son," they heard suddenly. They both turned around to see the King standing in the doorway, looking at them. "You make me very proud and I am sure you will be a great ruler once I retire." He moved closer to the two men, looking at them with a friendly smile on his face.

"I know now what to do and the three of us need to talk. This is not the place to talk about it, though. Let's go to my chambers. There are important matters you two need to know about."

CHAPTER 6

Spells and Sentries

The party was already on their way. The King had written the letter telling the Emperor to turn his army around and go home. *We do not want to fight, but if we have to, we will, with all our might*, the letter said.

Now the King knew he was right to say that in the letter. The Book told him what he had to do. Should the Emperor choose to go back, their lives will continue just like before. But the chances of that happening were very small. The King knew that. He understood that once the Emperor started on the road of conquering and pillaging, there would be nothing to stop him. Least of all a letter that told him to turn back! But he needed time to prepare and sending the messengers with the letter was a good way to stall him as any.

It was time for somebody to stop him and now he knew that they had the power to do it. Their sacrifice would defeat the Emperor and save all from his tyranny. If only he could plan everything right. As he was thinking about what he read just a short time ago, he led the two men into his private study. He invited them to sit and started.

"Ages ago, after land had separated from water, and rivers, planes and mountains were coming into being, countless creatures, all living in peace, roamed the lands. They all shared the food and water and all that the land had to offer. People were all living together as brothers and sisters and were working the land that provided them with everything they needed.

But one day, the sun disappeared behind big dark clouds and rain started to fall. It rained for so long that rivers started to swell and everybody had to look for safety on higher grounds. After countless days, rain has finally stopped and soon after, the land started to clear. But what was left behind was a muddy, deserted land. The food was scarce and clean water was not enough for everybody. Some decided to go look for other places that would provide for their families and that is when our forefathers left their native lands.

They travelled for many years, looking for a place where they would start their new lives. Finally, they arrived on these plains and decided to settle down. They looked around to see if others lived here, but they couldn't find anybody. The surroundings were beautiful, with rich land where they would grow crops to feed their families. The rivers had plenty of water, the forests had enough wood for their houses. So, in time, the people started to move farther and farther away from their first settlement, taking over more and more land, as nobody else came to claim it.

Not long after our forefathers' departure, as food was becoming scarcer and scarcer, back in the old homeland others decided to leave too. Some that strayed away arrived to the lands that our great-grandparents settled on and when they saw how rich the land was, they tried to take over some of the villages. Our forefathers, the Bird people, were kind and peaceful and did not like violence. They only wanted to work their lands and look after their families without having to worry about invaders. So, once they settled, they asked for the help of their Ancestors to protect them and they put a powerful spell in place to protect their sons and daughters from danger.

The spell would not prevent anyone from crossing onto their lands, as long as they would come in peace. But as vagabonds and looters tried crossing the borders thinking of pillaging the villages at the border, they were turned into stones. Frightened, not understanding what was happening, some of them tried to turn back. Only very few were able to cross back though. Those who managed to turn around, magically forgot all about the kingdom and what had happened to their companions.

The spell was such that should any of the Bird-people ever leave the lands, they, too, would forget who they were, where the kingdom was and who their Ancestors were. They would only remember everything again when the kingdom would be in grave danger.

In time, the secret turned into a great burden for the rulers of the Bird-people. The spell was safe as long as only the rulers of the land knew about it. The secret would be only passed on to the heir upon his or her coronation, so the secret would be kept safe. The new ruler would have to pledge never to tell anybody about it. When it was my turn to take over from my father," the King explained, "I took the same pledge, but it has been so long since I did that, that I almost forgot about it and the details of the spell were never shared by my father, as he did not remember them either."

His father had just told him that the spell would be in jeopardy only if the kingdom itself was threatened by large armies of invaders. Should an invasion be imminent, then the only way to save the country was to get all the Bird-people together again. With all their united powers they would defeat the enemy. But once they did that, their lives would be changed forever. They would lose their land forever and would be forced to scatter around the world, not being able to tell anybody about their sacrifice. They would never remember who they were and they could never return to their native lands.

Myrdall, Rehon and their companions had been travelling for a long time and the horses needed to rest, as the men did too. They had crossed the border only a day ago and the land ahead of them looked burned and deserted. They stopped the horses on top of a hill as soon as they could see the camp and let them graze on the browning grass. They sat down to eat from the satchels tied to their saddles. The Emperor's camp was down in the valley—larger than they expected.

"Do you think he will want to talk to us, Rehon?" asked Myrdall looking at the long line of tents. "He must have his mind already set on conquering everybody, why would he listen to us?"

"He knows that if he cannot go past us, he cannot go on with his madness," answered his friend lost in thought. Then, pulling himself together, turned to the Captain.

"We should sent Fardran and Gandar ahead to let him know we are coming and ask him to meet with us. When they are finished with their meal, send them over. We'll follow shortly."

He stood up and took a few steps to stretch his legs. His friend followed him and both looked at the camp in the valley.

"They are so many. Too many . . ." he said to himself and headed back to the horses. Hesitating and still looking at the camp in the valley, Myrdall asked. "Do you think your Father will go to war if the Emperor does not turn away?" He did not wait for his friend's answer and went on.

"I hope to see Llewella before we go to battle and ask her to marry me. I have been thinking about building her a house by the river, but now, I am not sure it is possible anymore . . ." He stopped abruptly and turned his back to his friend ashamed he betrayed his secret. He finally turned to face his friend who was staring at him, surprised. The awkwardness of the moment passed and Rehon grabbed his friend's arm and gave him a big hug, patting him on the back. Laughing, he continued.

"You never said anything about you and Llewella. And come to think of it, she didn't say anything about you either. You, marry my sister?" He suddenly stopped and minding himself, smiled and looked at Myrdall again, who was now looking down, somewhat ashamed of his high hopes.

"You need to go and ask her hand from Father, you know. She is a princess, and you need to ask Father first, that's the law. You scoundrel, why didn't you say . . ."

He stopped suddenly as he saw Randalf, the Captain of the guards running towards him.

"What is it Captain?" Not stopping, Randalf pointed to the camp, shouting.

"Fardran and Gandar have arrived at the camp, My Lord, and the Emperor's guards are holding them at the entrance." Worried, looking at the two men, he continued. "My Lords, we need to hurry. Something is happening." He turned and went back running to get the horses. Rehon moved closer to his friend and, smiling, patted him again on the back.

"We will talk more about this. Now we need to see what is going on. Let's go!" he called out to the party, as he mounted his horse and started on their way to the camp. There was commotion around the gates and more soldiers were coming out of their tents. *Yes, something was happening,* thought Rehon, *hopefully, nothing bad . . .*

The King stopped as if to rest a little and stood up. His two most trusted people were in the room with him, learning about their Ancestors. They were both sitting quietly in their chairs not daring to move. All of it was overwhelming and now that he was thinking about it, he had needed some time to take it in, too, when he first read it.

The Spirit had told him all that happened in the centuries after their settlement, but that was not the important part. He felt he had to skip to the tasks that his son and the Councillor had to fulfill, but he also felt it was equally important for them to understand why they had to do that. He sat down again and continued.

"After centuries of living in peace and prosperity, some of the Bird people decided to go explore other lands, to meet other people. In time, word of their deeds and courageous acts started to travel around. Stories started to be written and songs were sung about their bravery and kindness. They would be honoured guests everywhere they went and everyone wanted to have them at their table.

After centuries of roaming around the world, some of the descendants of the travelers decided to settle down. They started building homes for their families. All of this time, none of them remembered who their forefathers were and where they had come from, and so they lived good and long lives in their new settlements. The spell that protected the kingdom had erased their memories and they did not know anything about the Bird Kingdom.

Only for some time now, the Elders started to have visions they could not explain. People started to get together, to talk about how to return "home". The spirits of the Ancestors found out about the troubles with the Emperor and started talking to them, telling them to wait for messengers who will guide them back home."

The King stopped again and looking at the two men sitting in his study, finished. "Bird people everywhere started to remember who they were and have started sending messengers to each other. Parties from all lands where they now live are meeting and talking about sending a messenger to the palace, soon. We need to welcome all Bird people back home, my friends. We need to save our peoples and everybody else from the Emperor and only *we* can do that."

CHAPTER 7

The Emperor

Centuries ago, in the land of Bridd, the people lived happy lives without the fear of war or famine. Year after year, the crops were good and every fall, the Harvest Festival brought people from across the land to celebrate and thank the land and sky.

This year, like the years before, old man Gumpen was picking up the last pumpkins from the field around the house. He soon would fill the last cart and head for the Festival down in the village of Ronda. The pumpkins were ready to be cleaned and he called his sons to help him hoist the bigger ones in the cart. His arms were not as strong as they used to and he had been depending more and more on his eldest son.

Finup had grown up to be the stubby, strong man his father always wished for in his heir. Gumpen hoped he would be ready to look after their lands when he would go to the Ancestors. His eldest son enjoyed working the fields but lately he has started complaining about why nobody visited them anymore. *All they had been doing for as long as they could remember*, he was saying bitterly, *was planting the fields in the spring and harvesting the crops in the fall. He wanted to go to other places and meet other people.*

Life in Nill had become very boring in the years past and like him, other young people were thinking of leaving the village and travel to meet others. The Elders were trying to talk them out of it, only to make them even more determined to leave.

Everything was ready for the festival and early next morning they would be on their way. Rubana, Gumpen's wife came out of the house and looked at the filled carts.

"Another good crop this year, husband. We should get good money for it. We will need to buy meat for the winter and straw for the animals." She turned to Finup who was loading the last basket of corn in one of the carts.

"Maybe in spring we will thank the Ancestors for a good wife to help me with the work in the house, what do you think, Finup?"

The young man looked at his mother sadly and mumbled.

"We'll see, Mother, we'll see." He continued bitterly, not looking up at his parents. "There are no *good* girls in the village and the Elders don't allow us to leave Nill. How are we going to have a family if we are not allowed to choose our wives ourselves?" He dropped the basket in the cart and turned to his father.

"I have asked you to let me go to Ronda to meet with Marden and his friends, but you would not allow it. There is nobody here in Nill that I can talk to, there is nothing for me to do here, except to dig the ground and load up carts for the Festival. Father, you need to let me go! I want to learn about other places, I want to go see the King's palace and maybe become a soldier in his guard."

Since his father did not say anything, he turned and looked at his mother.

"I beg you Mother, I beg you, let me go. I promise I will return and help you with the crops every fall. I want you to be proud of me." His mother looked down and covered her mouth. It wasn't *she* who wouldn't allow her eldest son to go away and she understood him, as she remembered of times when she felt cut off from the world. But the Elders of the village did not approve of that and Finup hated them and the law.

"One day, I *will* leave and I will *never* come back. I hate this place, I hate the law that keeps us tied to this land. And I am not the only one who thinks like this," he shouted kicking the dust and looking angrily at his parents.

Finup woke up early, before the sun was up. Today was the day. The crops were in the barns and winter was in the air. He had packed his few things without saying anything to his parents and has been keeping them hidden in the barn. He has been ready to leave his home and family for a long time now. The sun started to climb up in the sky as he was getting dressed. He needed to be quiet—he couldn't risk his father catching him. He would meet two of his friends on the road to Ronda, the neighbouring village. Other young men and women from that village would join them later and together would go out in the world to find adventure. They have been secretly meeting for the past months and last time, they decided that today was the day they would leave everything and everybody behind.

The closer the Emperor and his army were getting to the land of Bridd, the bigger grew his bad feeling about taking over that land. There was something about that place that he could not explain, that has been making him want to turn around. His trusted General Gampill had disagreed with him and laughed at his fears. He insisted they kept going. *There is nothing special about this land, except maybe they would want to put up a bit of a fight*, he said, mockingly. But the Emperor knew that was not it.

A few weeks ago he started having these dreadful dreams that would wake him up in the middle of the night, covered in sweat. The dream would start with him being somewhere that appeared to be *home*, working the land and helping load carts with pumpkins, corn and other vegetables. Sweat would drip over his eyes and his father would laugh happily at the sight of the good crops. Then the farmhouse would change into a palace surrounded by well groomed gardens but he could not remember where that was. He then would find himself flying over some land and from above he would see his *father* covered in blood lying on the ground and his old farm house in flames. Down, in front of the house, he would see a short, stubby man cackling over more bodies covered in blood, spread around on the ground and one of them was . . . his own. He would wake up screaming, afraid to go back to sleep. And the nightmare would repeat again and again as soon as he would fall asleep.

The emissaries slowed down as they approached the entrance to the camp. The men dismounted and stopped to watch what all the commotion was about. Their horses were restless, hooves were hitting the ground and the men could hardly hold them steady. A soldier dressed in a shiny armour, looked at them from afar and moved closer. He nodded to a couple of soldiers dressed in brown uniforms, who pushed the two messengers forward. Both Fardran and Gandar looked at their captain and then at the King's son and started to say something, only to be brutally interrupted by the man who seemed to be in charge.

"These two say you are here to see His Lordship, is that true? Who are you and what do you want?" His voice was booming and when he talked the scar that covered half of his left cheek moved up and down making him as hideous, as he sounded mean. The armour he was wearing was shiny and covered with what looked like medals. He had taken off his helmet and his dark hair was long and carefully braded at the back. He looked arrogant and menacing and they could tell that the others feared him.

Rehon stepped forward and looked him in the eye.

"I am Rehon of Bridd and I come to bring a message to your lord from my father, King Lade-Gleal. We ask you to turn around and leave our lands. We do not wish to fight you, go back to your lands and no harm will come to you."

At first, there was an eerie moment of silence. Nobody moved, even the wind seemed to have stopped to listen to the young man. Then, a crooning sound filled the air and nobody could tell where it was coming from. But soon, they realised it was the armoured man, he was laughing, only his laughter sounded more like the grinding of two stones in a blacksmith's shop. His mouth was closed and the sound came out through his nose and that made it sound non-human. Almost immediately, the other soldiers realised what was happening and joined in the surreal laughter, the noise roaring over their heads. After a few moments that felt like minutes, the soldier held his hand up and everybody stopped as suddenly as they started.

"You want us to turn around and leave, you say? Just like that?" The soldiers looked at him again not knowing if they should start their monstrous cackling again, but nothing in his attitude said so, so they kept silent.

"Do you know who I am, you insignificant creature? I am *the* General Gampill, the General who slashed the heads on fifty cowards in one strike. My army has been invincible ever since we have started cleaning the world of insignificant creatures like you and we will not stop now because you say so." He raised his arm and the cackling started again, now louder and stronger than before, only now the faces of the soldiers were filled with fear.

As the roaring went on, Myrdall moved toward Gampill. His fists were clenched and he was reaching for his sword. Rehon saw the movement and stopped his friend before he could get to the general. The roaring stopped suddenly as the General raised his arm again, although some voices could still be heard coming from the back of the crowd.

Silence fell over the valley and Rehon reached into his satchel and grabbed his father's letter. It was bearing the Bridd seal—an eagle with spread wings holding a scepter in his claws—and he showed it to the General who reached out his gloved hand to grab it. Rehon smiled proudly and retracted his hand not allowing him to touch it.

"Only the Emperor can see this, *General*," he said. "You are merely his servant. Let your master know why we are here. The sooner I give this to him, the sooner we will be on our way."

Silence filled the air once again, but the General did not argue this time, and clenching his teeth only nodded towards an older soldier, heavily armed, who had been standing on the side, not participating in the mocking of the messengers. He quickly headed toward a large tent in the middle of the camp. A pair of soldiers dressed in golden armours met him as he was getting closer. The old man said something to them and one of them went inside the tent, only to return a few moments later. He then turned and waved at the General who put his helmet back on and walked towards the tent. Without looking at them, he gestured to the group to follow and a path started to form.

As they were approaching the tent, some of the soldiers stopped what they were doing and joined the crowd as they were walking past. They were not wearing the armours the commanders who met them did. They did not seem to be regular soldiers. Their clothes were tarnished and their weapons old and rusty. Myrdall looked at his friend and whispered.

"He has taken people prisoners and turned them into soldiers in his army. That's how he can keep fighting." Rehon only nodded and kept walking toward the tent.

They stopped a few steps away from it and one of the guards rushed to hold the reins of their horses as they headed toward the entrance. The cloth door was suddenly pulled open from the inside and a small antechamber appeared. The two young men entered while everybody else waited outside.

The news of the emissaries from the kingdom of Bridd spread amongst the emperor's army. Some soldiers moved silently closer and watched the group heading for the tent. Everybody was watching them and even the captains moved closer, pushing the curious soldiers aside to see them better. At the back of the crowd, an older man, in a tattered uniform, blood dried on his armour, gestured to a group that came closer. They all looked around, making sure nobody noticed their movement and the old man whispered.

"These are the Bridd emissaries. I wonder why they are here. They will not give up without a fight, I know that, but it was a bad idea to come here in the devil's den and challenge him. Let everybody know about it and tonight we will meet when everybody will be sleeping." The men nodded quietly and joined the crowd. The old man returned to polishing his sword.

Tonight is the night, he said to himself, *when we will let them know about us.*

Rehon walked first through the cloth door, followed by Myrdall. The General waited outside with the older soldier and the guards. The small antechamber was draped with furs and jewellery, making it obscene in its opulence. Another cloth door swung open and a much larger room, also filled with trophies met the two men. A man that looked like a servant gestured them in and as they entered, he left the room quietly. They lowered their heads as they went in and stopped in front of an empty throne, also adorned with precious stones and lined with furs. A raspy voice called and they turned to see a short, stubby man, dressed in golden gowns. On his shoulders, a purple cape sparkled with more jewels. On his head, a grotesque crown was holding back a ruffle of black hair.

"What do you want," he shouted. "Who are you?" Rehon moved forward and took his father's letter out from his satchel once more.

"I am Rehon, son of King Lade-Gleal, the master of the land of Bridd. This is Myrdall, son of Brohan, First Councillor. I bring you a letter from my Father, asking you to turn your army around and leave. We do not wish to fight you. We are peaceful people and never had to fight any wars, but if we have to, we will, with all our might." He stopped, looking at the Emperor, waiting for his answer.

"King Lade's son, you say," he asked pretending to be lost in thought. "And this is the First Councillor's son? People say your father must be about 100 years old by now, am I right?" he asked Rehon but not waited for him to answer. "He does not want to fight me? Does he want to surrender without fight?" he continued, pretending he did not hear what Rehon had said. "You wouldn't be the first ones, you know," he continued smirking. "Many other kings just surrendered, they were not prepared to fight and word of my army and its might may have had something to do with that." Suddenly he started cackling, just like his General minutes ago and the two men cringed.

"How dare you come to me and tell me to turn around?" he bellowed suddenly, his eyes filled with anger. "Have you not heard of the Great Emperor Finup? I am the most feared man in the lands from the Great Water to the Deep Marshes and the High Mountains! Nobody tells me what to do! Nobody tells me to turn back!"

His voice echoed as the two looked at him with some sort of pity, not fear. That made the Emperor even angrier. He had expected them to be afraid, not defiant. He had met others in his tent, but they all had come there to humbly surrender. These two, well, with them it was different and he could not figure out what. The moment they stepped into his tent, the bad feeling he has been having came back stronger than before. A nagging thought that this battle was not going to be as easy, was making his head throb. Looking at their demeanour, he shivered and felt like he just woke up from one of the nightmares he has been having lately. He could not explain why he felt anger about their presence but also some sort of excitement at seeing them. He tried to cover his mixed feelings by crossing his arms on his chest and looking at them menacingly.

"This is the letter that my father sends you," Rehon started all of a sudden and his voice made the Emperor jump at his words. "Read it and let us know what your answer is. We will wait on the hill close to your camp. Should we not hear back from you by sunset, we will take it that you don't want to turn around and leave. Then we'll head back to the palace and get ready to fight. We will wait until sunset," repeated Rehon and was about to turn around and leave.

"How dare you talk to me like that," the Emperor snarled, grabbing his arm, "you, a, a . . . nothing, an insignificant creature?" His voice was filled with an angry madness and his body cringed with fury. He looked at Rehon and spat the words.

"You go back to your, to your . . ." He stopped as if he couldn't find the words that would hurt him enough. ". . . to your pitiful father and tell him that Emperor Finup is ready for battle. He has been ready and will be ready to fight anybody who stands in his way. You go home and tell him that he has one week to get ready. Unless you send word you surrender," he mocked them again. "Now leave! I will see you on the battle field!"

Without opening the letter, he ripped it into pieces and threw it at the two emissaries. The pieces hit the two young men and fell on the floor, but they did not flinch. The looks on their faces showed pity and that infuriated the Emperor even more. His voice bellowed as he called the guards. The armoured men showed immediately and pushed the emissaries out of the tent. The crowd was still there, watching, waiting silently for something to happen. But nothing did and, somewhat disappointed, they started to go about their business.

Myrdall grabbed the reins of his horse and mounted it. Rehon followed and gestured the others to follow. Clouds of dust covered their tracks and there was no fast enough horse in the world to take them away from that awful place. They were heading home at the speed of their thoughts. Soon they will start preparing for battle.

CHAPTER 8

The Tasks

The King stopped for a moment to rest and looked at Gleal.

"I need your help, son. You need to go and find somebody who will help us defeat the Emperor. You will have to bring him here as fast as your horses will take you. Find Nevara and Keapock and bring them to the main hall. Take what you need for a long trip and tell the kitchens to pack you food and water. Here is the message to give to this man and this is how to find him. Safe travels, my son and be back soon." Without a word, Gleal stood up, bowed and left the room.

The King then turned to his Councillor. "Master Brohan, take the Chief of Guards and the palace's guard brigade and travel to the north borders. Here is the letter you need to give Ropettian, the leader of the Larmar people. You will be meeting him at the border. The Spirit told me that they are heading our way," he added quickly seeing the surprise on the man's face.

The King looked his friend in the eye and continued. "Meet our long lost family and bring them over to the city. Ride swiftly my friend." He shook his hand and Brohan left with a quick nod.

As soon as his son was on his way, the King went to the drawing room to look for his eldest daughter. Llewella was sitting on the window seat looking out lost in thought. She turned when she heard the footsteps and when she saw her father, stood up and smiled.

"How are you Father, you seem worried. What is it?" The King looked at her fondly and smiled back. How she reminded him of her mother—her voice, her smile, her walk.

"I need you to do something for me, my daughter. Soon, guests will come to visit us and we need to look after them like they are family. Have the guest rooms ready and tell the kitchens to prepare the festive meal. Send for the best wine from the cellars and have the cooks find the freshest fruit. Get your sister and friends and help set the tables in the Dining Hall—soon we will celebrate the return of our long lost brothers and sisters.

As she looked surprised at his words, he continued.

"As soon as Rehon and his party are back, everybody will find out the news and how we can save our land and our friends from the Emperor's tyranny." The young woman waited for her father to continue, but he did not and gently grabbed her hand.

"Go on, my dear, there is much for you to do. I have important things to do, too. We need to hurry. There is little time." He turned around and left the drawing room, while his daughter watched him disappear behind the big doors of the Throne Room.

The messengers were closing in on the palace and the horses were covered in white froth from the effort. Rehon and Myrdall were in the lead and their horses were showing signs of exhaustion. Rehon stopped his horse and called to a man standing on the side of the road watching the party getting closer.

"Do you have a horse of your own, good man?" Rehon asked him, dismounting.

"I need your horse," he shouted again as the man didn't seem to understand. He stopped in front of him and asked him one more time.

"Do you have a horse, old man?"

"I do, My Lord," the old man answered quickly pulling himself together, "but my horse is old. My son's horse is much faster and he lives just over there." He turned pointing at a house with burgundy trimmings.

"Bridon," he shouted, "Bridon, come here and bring your horse, my son, his highness needs it. Hurry, my son, hurry!"

A tall young man showed up and came running toward the party that now stopped. He moved closer to Rehon and as he recognised him, he bowed respectfully. "My horse will be ready in a moment, My Lord, my brother is going to bring it out. Do you need something to eat or drink?" Rehon smiled at the young man's offer, but shook his head. The man's younger brother appeared with the horse and Rehon grabbed the reins, mounting it. He tipped his helmet and resumed his gallop toward the palace.

The rest of the party grabbed the reins of their horses to steady them and prepared to follow their leader. Right then, the man's wife came out carrying a tray with food and a pitcher of water for the travellers. The tired soldiers looked at Myrdall for approval and with a smile, he nodded. The men grabbed the food and started gulping it down while the woman was filling their glasses. More women started to come out of their homes bringing food and refreshments for the travellers and the men grabbed the horses and led them to buckets of water. The entire street was now out and the men gathered around Myrdall serving him food and drinks.

"My Lord, my name is Bridon, son of Ronden. I see you have travelled far and are in a hurry to get back to the palace. What is the news that you carry, My Lord?" Myrdall looked at him and the other men not knowing if he should say anything.

"We bring news from the border, Bridon, we met with the Emperor who has been threatening to take over our land. Prince Rehon gave him a letter from our King and we are now back to tell the King the news." He stopped as the men were looking at him and finished.

"King Lade will make an announcement soon and everybody will know what to do. Now we need to head for the palace too. We thank you for your generosity, but we must leave." With that, he gestured to the soldiers who were finishing the food and mounted his horse. The others followed and waving to the people in the street, spurred the horses that sprinted toward the palace. The people started to return to their homes. Bridon and a few of the men looked worried after the party.

Then he shook his head and headed home. *It is not good news they are bringing*, he thought, *they would not be rushing like that without telling us anything.*

The King was headed to the dungeons once more. This time he needed to find out where the true heirs of the Bird people lived. It was the last task and he took it upon himself to complete it. It was he who will have to talk to them, as difficult as this was. All his life he believed that he and his father and their forefathers were the true descendants of the Bird people. But the *Book of Wisdom* was telling something else. More than that, he will have to tell this to his own people and he did not know how they would take it. His people trusted him and he was sure of their loyalty, but the news of the Emperor moving closer to their borders, together with the news that others may claim their land, well, that could be too much to take. He, himself was uncomfortable thinking that he may have to give up the reins of the kingdom and move out of the palace. But if it was to come to this, he was certain his family would understand.

He arrived at the small passage he had crossed only a few days ago and once more opened the door. The lights came on just like last time and he put the torch down by the door. The Book was waiting for him on the same table and as he moved closer, it opened and the pages started to shuffle again. They stopped and the Book was now opened at the beginning. *How it All Began*, it read. He took a deep breath, sat down in the small chair and started reading.

A long time ago, there lived three brothers, well respected and trusted by their people. When the Big Floods came, they took their people to higher grounds and kept them safe until the waters receded. But soon they realised that the food will not be enough for everybody, so the oldest brother, Toran Bird decided to leave with those ones who wanted to join him and go look for a better place to live. His younger brothers were worried about his decision but they too knew that soon they would have to leave these deserted lands.

Toran Bird and his companions wandered for many years until they finally arrived to a place with rich lands and clean rivers. They decided to settle there and started building homes with wood from the forests not far away and roads with rocks from the river beds. They started working the land and soon the crops were more than enough to feed them. What was left, they stored for winter. They named the land the Kingdom of Bird and later Toran Bird took the name of King Bird.

Soon after their departure, the younger brother, Toran Mordon, decided to leave too: the land couldn't offer enough for everybody and his people were going hungry. They packed their few belongings and went after his older brother. But faith took them to other parts of the world and they settled in a place surrounded by tall rugged mountains, crossed by deep fast rivers and called it Mortoria.

Life was not getting any better for those who stayed behind and the third brother, Toran Kostan, decided to take his people away, hoping he would meet his brothers again. Life took them even farther apart and the land where they settled was covered by large fields, where grass was growing tall, swaying in the warm wind. Wide rivers were crossing them and they settled there, calling the place Larmar.

The three Toran brothers had inherited their parents' wisdom and kindness and that made them very much liked and trusted by their followers. Before their father Toran passed away and went to meet the Ancestors, they all received gifts that were to be kept safe from strangers. The eldest son got a dagger with precious stones encased in its hilt and a set of necklaces; Mordon, the second son, got a beautiful emerald ring and Kostan, a priceless purple gem. They were told that together, the gifts had magnificent powers, but when separated, each was only a valuable heirloom.

The other tale they were told was that the heirlooms would let its owner know if their siblings, or their descendants, were in need of help. When that would happen, the precious stones on the hilt would fade, the necklaces would be covered in rust, the emerald would crack and the gem would turn black. When this happened, should they go looking for their brothers, the stones would regain their shine and the gold would shed its blemishes. As they got closer to each other, the gems would shine more brightly and the gold would turn the purest orange colour.

Ever since they had been in Toran's possession nobody needed to use their powers so nobody actually knew the kind of powers the possessions had as the only person who had that knowledge, the Protector, was now long gone. He had written about the secret powers of each of the gifts and the scrolls were hidden away to help keep them safe. He had put the scrolls in a safe place that was protected by magic and only a true heir of Toran's could get to them. Toran himself did not know where the scrolls were kept, but he had asked the Protector to give him clues as where they were hidden. The Protector told him that the clues were in fact riddles that only he or his heirs would be able to answer.

Time had passed and King Bird forgot about his gifts as they were placed in his castle's vault for safe keeping. On a shelf in the dungeons, the gifts were gathering dust. One day, the King went looking for some old decrees down in the old library and a strange feeling made his heart jump when he entered the room. He thought nothing of it until he noticed a small chest on one of the shelves that looked familiar. He took it off and the contact with the wood brought a flashback of a memory: an old man giving him a bundle wrapped in a cloth. The wood the chest was made of felt fragile and he opened it carefully not to damage it and then he saw them: the bundle in his flashback. He unwrapped it and uncovered two golden necklaces and a dagger. The necklaces looked shiny and new, but the gems on the hilt of the dagger had lost their shine.

King Bird wondered what had happened to them and then he remembered about his father telling him and his brothers the tale of the four gifts and how they would tell about the welfare of the other brothers. He tried to remember who the dagger told about, but could not. He tried to remember anything about the gifts but all that happened too long ago. As the uneasy feeling disappeared when he closed the chest he thought that maybe the stones on the dagger faded because of the passing of the time—after all the necklaces looked fine. He put the chest back on the shelf, promising himself to try find out more about the heirlooms later.

The King stopped reading and stood up. He rubbed his eyes and looked around in the room. He didn't remember anything about a chest or a dagger: his father may have forgotten to tell him about it or he didn't know about them at all. This seemed to have happened a long time ago and just like the knowledge about the Bird King that had been lost for so long, maybe the tales about the gifts were lost too. But just in case they were not a legend, he looked around to see if the chest was still there—the Book said that his forefather had left the gifts in the dungeons and he had been living in the same palace that he had build centuries ago. He checked the shelves carefully. They were now filled with books and parchments and he did not know when the chest had been places there. Maybe the chest had rotted and the cloth turned to dust and there was nothing to find after all. But he had a feeling that the necklaces and the dagger were still here and that made him keep looking.

Then he stopped in his tracks and realised what the Book was talking about: the necklace was the one he had inherited from his father and his wife had been wearing when she was alive and that his son Gleal had taken to old man Gumpen. But the Book talked about *two* necklaces, where could the second one be? And where was the dagger? He did not remember seeing it. Who would know where it was? He returned to the Book and continued reading, but there was no mention of the gifts in the following pages. The chapter only told the history of his Ancestors and listed their names. There was the mention of the creation of the villages of Nill and Ronda, about his great-grandfather and how the name of the kingdom was changed from Bird to Bridd. Nothing about the other gifts or where they could be!

The King left the book and called the Spirit, but he did not answer. Then he realised how late it must have been and that maybe his people would be looking for him so he grabbed the torch and returned upstairs. He knew now what his new task was: to find the gifts and the scrolls with the riddles. He could be the one to solve them and turn on the magic in them. He did not know why, yet, but he hoped he will find that out when he found them.

Right now, he had to get everything ready for the arrival of his brothers and sisters and plan the defeat of the Emperor.

CHAPTER 9

Nill

Gleal and his party were getting closer to the village of Nill. They have passed through many cities and towns. The people would welcome them and asked them to enjoy their hospitality, but they had to keep going. They had to hurry to find this man, Gumpen. They had to bring him to the palace and Gleal had something his Father gave him that would persuade him to come. He did not know what it was, but the King said that when he saw it, he would understand how important it was for him to be at the palace. They hoped the man was still alive, he must be very old, as old as his father, if not older.

The two men who were accompanying him, Nevara and Keapock, were riding quietly. They were not used to long rides and the trip was taking a toll on them. Nevara was one of the Captain of the Guards' two sons and the youngest of his children. He was tall, like most of the Bridd people, with a tuft of red hair. His face was covered in freckles and the green eyes were shadowed by bushy eyebrows.

His friend Keapock, was Gleal's second cousin. His father and his late mother were first cousins and they were living just down the street from the palace. Keapock would come over to the palace when they were children and played in the garden or chased each other in the palace's halls, to his mother's exasperation. He took after his father—the dark curly hair was held back by the helmet. He looked very young, like a teenager, although he was only a few years younger than Gleal. They were both men of little words and Gleal had suffered during the trip for not having a companion to talk to.

They were getting closer to Nill and Nevara called him, asking if they should stop and let the horses rest.

"We are close now, Nevara, we might as well keep going. There is an inn in the village where we can stop and have some food before we go looking for the old man. The people there may know if he is still around or where he lives." They spurred the horses that started in a quick trot.

Rubana was sitting on a bench in front of the house looking at people walking by, greeting them. They greeted her back and that made her feel good. That was Gurmup, her neighbour's son—what a handsome young man he turned out to be. His wife was expecting their second child and that made old Barnam very proud. They still lived in his father's house, as many young men in their village were, and they looked after the parents who in return looked after their grandchildren.

There was Lindulla, her son's sister-in-law. She was coming back from Ronda, where she had her family. She was living there and from time to time she would come over to Nill to help look after her sister's children. Rubana's son, Soban, had three children and they needed all the help they could get. The young woman waved at her and she waived back.

She and Gumpen on the other hand, did not have any help. Her only daughter married and moved away to Hortoll with her husband's family. They would come to visit on her birthday or for the Harvest Festival, but even then they only stayed for a few days—Hortoll was far away and it took them two whole days to get back home.

She did have another son, but he was dead now. He had left one day and never returned. Her oldest son and their hope, Finup, was gone and they had no help now that they were old and lonely. She had cried for a long time and prayed that he would come back, but after a while she had given up and they buried him—an empty coffin—and moved on. Now she was sitting here all alone watching the people passing by, thinking about her life and her children.

Gumpen, her husband has been sick for a long time and he too, missed having a son to help them, to look after them. He would lie in bed all day, looking out the window, not talking to her or to anybody. He would not talk to her about Finup or Soban or their daughter. He blamed himself for Finup's leaving Nill and he blamed the law that forced the young people stay in the village. After that day, after Finup and many other young men and women left the village and never returned, they had changed the law, but it had been too late. Too many parents were left with broken hearts and too many families without help. They only hoped that when their time would come, they would go to the Ancestors to join Finup.

The inn was clean and the people looked friendly. The inn keeper greeted them and showed them to their rooms. They had travelled for a long time and Gleal wished he would have time to rest. But his father told him that there was no time and they had to find the old man and bring him to the palace. He told his two companions to get some rest and went back down in the main hall to talk to the innkeeper, maybe he knew Gumpen and could show him where he lived.

The inn was full of people and he had to navigate through the tables to find the man. He found him behind the bar serving hot drinks to his customers. Gleal sat down on one of the tall stools and asked for a mug of hot cider. The long ride and the cold wind got him chilled to the bone, so a hot drink might help him warm up.

The innkeeper smiled and asked if he could offer him something to eat with the drink, but Gleal smiled back.

"Thank you for the drink, it will warm me up. I am here to look for an old man by the name of Gumpen. Do you know where he lives?" The keeper stopped with the pint in his hand and turned to look closer at the stranger.

"I do know where he lives, but why are you asking about him? What do you want with him? Are you in some sort of trouble?"

Gleal looked puzzled at the keeper and returned the question. "Why would I be in trouble?" The man looked again at Gleal and in a low voice said again.

"Yes, I know where he lives but he is old and not well. Why are you looking for him?" Gleal thought it was time he told the man who he was and was just about to do that when someone behind him tripped over his chair falling over the bar. In his fall he broke the prince's pint that spilled the cider over his cloak. The prince stood up and took the soaked cloak off his shoulders. His embroidered coat showed and suddenly silence fell in the room.

"Your highness," said the keeper, realising who he had been talking to, "forgive me for my rudeness. There is not often we have people come here asking questions about our Elders." He rushed from behind the bar and helped the prince clean himself up. He then nodded to a woman who quickly went in the back and returned with a plate filled with meats and bread and a clean pint with more steaming hot cider.

She gestured to a pair who was sitting at a table in the corner of the room and they stood up quickly taking their mugs with them. The woman set everything on the empty table and grabbed a chair for the guest. Making a path between the stunned customers she invited him to sit down.

The keeper pushed some of the curious aside and moved closer to Gleal.

"Gumpen is not well, My Lord, he has been sick for a very long time. What does your highness need with him?" Gleal thought that maybe he should talk with the keeper in a more private place, so he asked him to bring the food to his room. He stood up and went back upstairs. The innkeeper and his wife followed him.

"My father, King Lade needs Gumpen at the palace as soon as possible," started Gleal as soon as they were inside. "The old man can help defeat the Emperor and my father needs to talk to him about something that happened a long time ago." The two villagers looked at each other and the woman spoke for the first time.

"My Lord, Gumpen is very old and very ill, he cannot travel. There has to be another way to defeat the Emperor." Gleal looked at them and understood what the two meant: if the faith of the kingdom rested with Gumpen's going to the city of Bridd, then they were as good as lost.

CHAPTER 10

Premonitions

The King stopped reading and rubbed his eyes. His head was pounding and as he tried to absorb all that he read, a feeling of helplessness filled his heart. Here he was once again reading from the *Book of Wisdom*. He needed to find out who the true heirs of the Bird people were and so far the story did not give him any clues. He needed to find out the dagger and the second necklace and what their powers were. What he had been reading so far told him about the beginning of his peoples and the Book had recorded every detail about the big rains, the floods and the departure.

He forced himself to continue and tried to turn the pages ahead so he could get to the part he was interested in. But he could only turn one page at a time, so he realised that as unimportant as it all sounded so him, he had to read it all, page by page. That angered him: he would have loved to read about the beginnings of his kingdom, but there was no time for that now. The Book apparently, did not think so.

Annoyed, the King tried one more time to turn the pages without reading, but the Book would not allow that and he stood up angrily, looking around. He started talking, at first more to himself, pacing around, mumbling, and then louder, hoping that the Sprit that had greeted him every time, would hear him and help him get to the part that hc needed. "You know we don't have time for this! I need to get to the part that tells me how to find the true heirs of King Bird. Why can't I skip to that part? Why is the Book not letting me turn the pages without reading them?"

He waited, hoping the Spirit would answer. Nothing happened, though. Nobody answered and he got even more frustrated. He tried to pry the book off the table and like before, it did not budge. He lookcd around for something to help him do that and except for the torch, there was nothing else in the room but the books and parchments neatly arranged on the shelves.

"Spirit, I need your help. My kingdom is about to be taken over by the Emperor and I need to gather all my brothers and sisters if we want to defeat him."

The fact that the Spirit ignored him made him very angry but he realised there was nothing he could do about it. As he was heading back to the table to continue reading, a noise made him turn around. He hadn't noticed that small window before. It was covered in cob webs and somewhat hidden by a pile of parchments stacked on the floor. It was weird to see it—he knew that the room was under the ground, so curiously he pushed them aside. He thought the noise was coming from the other side of the window and as he got closer, the noise grew louder. It sounded like rushing water and he could not understand where the water would be coming from. He knew there were no springs or wells around the castle.

The window started to shake gently and a golden liquid started to seep in. It glowed as it was running down the wall and the King touched it with his fingers. It felt warm to the touch and soft like silk. It soothed him as it run over his hand and he put his other hand in it. Then suddenly, great pain shot through his arms and he withdrew them. He looked at the liquid and then back at his hands and saw that it had been absorbed into the skin. His hands were now a glowing golden colour. He tried wiping them on his clothes, but the liquid had dried out and would not come off. Suddenly, the glowing started to spread up the arms and as it did, the pain got once again insufferable. He screamed in agony and fell on his knees clutching his arms that were now throbbing. Still on his knees, he felt warmth wrapping his body and the pain suddenly changed to a soothing feeling. Now that the pain was gone, he stood up looking puzzled at his glowing arms.

And then he saw the transformation. His arms were not arms anymore, but wings, covered by greyish light feathers. Amazed, he looked at them turning to full grown wings and did not understand what was going on. Then, he felt something happening to his face. He could not tell what it was and there was no mirror for him to look into, but he could tell his nose was changing shape and his mouth was getting smaller. He tried to touch it with his arms, now completely covered by feathers and all he could feel was something hard and pointy.

He started moving back to the chair to sit down, as he started to feel dizzy, but his legs would not move and he stumbled. Reaching forward to steady himself, he looked down and saw why he could not move: his feet were not there anymore, but instead two claws were holding his body which now felt lighter. Struggling to keep his balance, the King forced himself to walk and instead, he took off floating gently above the floor. His arms were now spread to the sides and as he tried to move forward, something feeling like a natural instinct made him move them up and down. As he was doing that, he noticed the distance to the floor was growing bigger and for a moment he panicked. He was moving up steadily and that made him want to flap his arms faster. He could now see the library in its entirety. As he was soaring in the air, the books were getting smaller and the parchments resembled stacks of toothpicks. From the top of the room he suddenly realised what was happening: he was flying!

The planes surrounding the city were getting closer and from above, the land looked like perfect squares, lined by dark rows contouring what looked like gardens and fields.

'I am home, I am finally home,' thought the man and veered to find the castle. 'There it is, it looks just as I remember it. And there are the stables and the gazebo. Nothing has changed!' He was getting closer and closer to the land and soon he touched the hard ground.

'Everything seems so big!' he thought again looking around. 'And where is everybody?' Something did not seem right and he tried to move, but his walk felt more like hopping. What was wrong with his legs? He looked down and saw some strange things that did not look like his legs. They looked like . . . claws? What has happened to his legs? He lifted his arms and instead, he saw wings covered by lightly coloured feathers. Looking around, he saw a well with a trough beside it. A little bit of water was still on the bottom. 'The horses must have been drinking from it,' he thought again and headed over, struggling to keep his balance. He looked in the water and saw a reflection that made him jump: a small head

covered by feathers and a small beak where a nose was supposed to be. Two beady eyes were staring back at him.

'WHAT IS HAPPENING TO ME?' he screamed.

Ropettian woke up covered in sweat and looked around to see where he was. To his left, his wife, Traciana, was sleeping turned on the side, away from him. *I had this nightmare again,* he thought, wiping his sweaty forehead. He has been having it for some time now. His father was having one too and so were the other Elders—only they were not calling them *nightmares* but *news* from the Ancestors and they were saying they were called back home. But they *were* home, this has been their home for as long as anybody could remember.

The Elders have been getting together almost every day for a month now to discuss the dreams and some were talking about leaving these lands. Where would they go, nobody really knew but lately, some of the men were seriously thinking about leaving Larmar to head west.

Today was the day when his wife would be blessed by the Elders for bringing another heir to the people of Larmar. He got up and looked at her again. She looked so beautiful in her serene sleep. The baby was not due for another few months, but tradition said the woman had to be honoured by special celebrations and that would happen tonight, after sunset.

The women would put on their best clothes and braid their hair in sophisticated hairdos. The men would put on the ceremonial attire and they would all bring a gift to the mother-to-be. The gift was meant to bring peace and prosperity to the parents and they had to keep it in the house until the baby was born. After that, they had to pass it on to other parents-to-be and so, most of the gifts have been to some parents many times and travelled around from family to family.

His job tonight was to bring Traciana out to meet the guests and to lead her down the street to the holy gathering place. They would all gather there to sing songs of thanks to the Ancestors and ask for their blessing.

He got dressed and went outside. The sky was perfectly blue with no clouds as far as he could see and the sun was just coming out over the forest in the distance. Birds were singing and insects were buzzing around. Spring was here and everybody was getting ready to work the land and plant next fall's crops. The village's herd was already on the pasture and he waved at the young boys looking after the animals. Later, he would have to get the horses out of the stables and go to the fields, too.

The sun was rising quickly in the sky and he returned to the house. Traciana was still sleeping, so he started the morning meal. Today, on her special day, he would bring her the food in bed. She will be busy all day with the preparations for tonight's celebrations, so at least she will not have to worry about him going to work without eating.

In the dungeons of the palace, King Leal woke up and stood up rubbing his eyes. What has happened to him? Was that a dream or was it real? He looked at his arms and touched his face but all he could see and feel was his old face and his arms covered by his silk shirt. What was the liquid that touched his body and changed him? Where did it come from? And why did he change into a bird and not into another creature?

As if the Spirit read his mind, he spoke for the first time since he had been down there.

"What you saw showed you what would happen if you went to war and how you and your people would change once the battle ended." He continued. "You are the heirs of the Bird people and the change would turn you back into what your ancestors were before they turned into what you are today."

The ring was burning his finger and he was trying to take it off but it felt like it had merged with the skin. He tried to shake it off but that didn't work either. Maybe if he could put his hand in water it would slide off easier. He looked around for the bucket of

water that he used for washing himself and saw it in the corner of the room. He stood up and put his hand in the water. At first, the water felt good, but after a while it started to burn his skin and he tried to take it out. Only the hand was stuck in the water, that now looked like honey and, instead of soothing his raw finger, it made his whole hand burn.

He screamed and hit the bucket with his foot, trying to spill the liquid, but that only made it worse: the bucket flew in the air and his hand separated from the wrist. He grabbed the stump with his good hand and shrieked in pain. Looking around for the bucket, he noticed a door and struggling, he headed for it, hoping that the cool air would stop the pain. He tried to open it but it was locked and he realised he did not have the key. Frantically, his hand throbbing with pain, he looked around for the key but it was nowhere to be found. He tried the pockets of his robe, but it was not there either.

He charged towards the door, hoping he could break it open, but the door didn't budge and his shoulder sent searing pain in his body: the bones in it were broken and his only good arm fell down limp. Enraged he could not get out, he screamed, trying to ignore the pain, but that did not help either. He looked around for something to break the door with, but there was nothing he could use, except for the bed and a big armoire in one of the corners of the room.

He spun around trying to find a way out and noticed a window that was not there before and he looked around again to see what he could use to break it. He wrapped his stump in a blanket and used it to hit the window but nothing happened. As he was trying to find something heavier to break the window, he saw bars appearing and he realised what the room actually was: his prison. He finally understood that he will not be able to get out, no matter what he did. He fell down on his knees and started sobbing. But then, the pain in the arms stopped all of a sudden and he looked at them to see what happened.

Shocked, he saw that instead of arms he now had two short stumps covered in black fluff. He tried to move them and he was able to, but they were so short he could only use them to balance himself. He tried to stand up and he managed it—with some difficulty—but his body felt different and he looked down to notice that his feet were now connected to a stubby body covered in black feathers. His feet were now webbed and he tried to move, but he could only waddle around the room. His stumpy arms helped him move and keep his balance but soon he felt like dropping on his stomach and slide around the room using his feet to push himself forward. The urge became stronger and he dropped down on the floor which was now made of ice and started sliding around. The feeling made him so happy that he felt like hollering, only the only sound that came out was a low honking. Scared, he looked at his reflection in the shiny floor and saw a large beak with two beady eyes that looked back at him. 'What happened to me?' he shrieked in his mind. 'What is the creature that is staring back at me?' Then the floor tilted and he slid helplessly down the ramp into the ice cold water at its end. The cold felt good and the pain and anxiety washed away. He was finally home and he stopped worrying.

CHAPTER 11

Blood Brothers

They had been away from their home and families for a long time now. He was trying not to think about that, but for some time in the past months, the people started to whisper behind his back and he could hear them talking about going back home. As soon as he was coming near them, they would stop talking and would pretend to have something to do. Even his best friend, Marden, was avoiding him and lately was only coming to visit for a short time, finding excuses to leave early.

The day they had left their homes and went on to find *adventure* was the happiest day of his life. He never imagined that so long after his secret departure he would miss his family. He tried very hard to make himself believe that their leaving was for the best, but there were times when he did have second thoughts. Every single man and woman that went away that morning did it for the good of the village and when they would be ready to go back they would all return and spent the rest of their lives around their parents.

For many years they had wandered from place to place, doing small jobs here and there to earn their meal and shelter, but now it was time for them to settle down. He heard that there was work in the capital city, Bridd and he, Marden, Rotin and a few others were heading there in the morning. The others decided to go to Bordor, a small village by the northern border and settle there. What worried him was that a few of them were thinking of going back to Nill and nothing could make them change their minds. Marden, one of the young men from Ronda who decided to come with him to Bridd, tried to persuade the others to join Finup and his team but he had no luck.

Before turning in for the night, they all said their good-byes and he wished they would someday meet again. Nobody knew what life would throw at them, but deep in his heart he hoped all the sacrifices they had made would not be for nothing.

The City of Bridd welcomed him and his companions. The city was like nothing they have seen before. It was summer when they arrived and the trees were flashing their green crowns offering shade to the visitors and the locals alike. For the tired travellers everything looked beautiful and as they were heading for the *Traveller's Inn* they looked around at the neat houses and clean streets. The people were greeting them with friendly smiles and they saw the large house ahead of them. The place was crowded and they had to make their way through the people to find the innkeeper.

"My name is Finup and these are my friends Rotin and Marden," he said to the man tending the bar. "Radmic of the village of Bordor told us about this place and he said you could help us find work in the city. We need a place to stay and we have money to pay for food. Can you help us?" The man looked at the three strangers and pointed them to the only not occupied table.

He called to a young woman in the back and she came out with some food and drinks and set them on the table in front of the men.

"They will need rooms to stay for the night," he told the woman and she nodded, heading for the stairs. "When you are finished eating, come up and I will show you to your rooms," she told the men and turned to go get the rooms ready.

The inn keeper sat down at the table with the travellers and looking at Finup and his companions shook his head.

"You had to leave your home and your parents to come to the Big City to look for work, after wondering for how many years? Some years ago, I got word from your father, Finup, asking everybody about his son. He felt you betrayed him with your leaving without saying good-bye and he has been blaming himself for all the sorrow and bitterness your Mother has held against him all these years. He thinks you are dead, you know that? *Everybody* thinks you *all* are dead, they even buried you," he said looking around at the men who were now quietly starring down at the full plates.

"You broke your Mother's heart when you left like that, Finup. She hoped you will be her help and bring home a bride to look after them when they would be old and weak. Now they have no help since your brother and sister have moved out with their families and left your folks all alone." The man stopped and looked at them again and his face showed some sort of understanding, but the bitterness in his voice said something else.

"We had to leave, Master Mantril, we felt trapped in Nill," started Finup and the others nodded quietly. "We tried to talk to the Elders, but nobody listened to us and we had to take our lives into our own hands. Everybody expected us to follow the ways of our fathers and grandfathers, but times have changed and we had to change too. I hear they are now allowing people to go and marry outside of Nill and after our departure other villages had followed suit. After all, we did not ask for something impossible, we only asked that we opened the doors to the village for others to come and for us to go. We had to pay a heavy price for leaving like that, but if I had to do it again, I would without hesitation." He stopped and looked around as the others nodded in agreement.

"Father Gumpen is not the only one to feel betrayed, Master Mantril," Marden spoke for the first time, "we felt that neither of our parents understood us and that is why we had to do something about it. Now we are here and this is our life now. We paid the price for the decision we made years ago and have moved on."

As soon as the emissaries left, the Emperor got dressed and went outside. His bad feeling about the battle with the kingdom of Bridd was growing and after the argument with the King's son, the nagging feeling this was a bad decision became even worse. He looked around at the camp and the sight of the soldiers looking after their duties calmed him a little. In the distance, he saw the hills covered by browning grass and somehow they looked familiar. Behind the camp there was the forest that offered them shelter and wood for the fires. That looked familiar too and the bad feeling came back, even stronger. And then, there were those rocks in the distance that from afar looked like silhouettes of people. They apparently bordered the kingdom and the rain and the wind had smoothed them into tall columns. The land around it was flat and there were no other rocks in the vicinity, so where did they come from?

Had he been here before? He was sure he did not, but something at the back of his mind was telling him differently. The river that crossed into the kingdom was now carrying leaves and sticks and suddenly a flashback of him playing on a river bank, skipping rocks and splashing happily with other children made him lose his balance and reach for thin air. Gampill, who followed him silently when he left the tent, caught him just in time and looked at him worried. The soldiers closest to them jumped on their feet to help their leader, but the General growled at them to mind their business. They moved away going back to their jobs and muttered something about wanting to help.

"My Lord, are you all right?" Gampill asked, guiding him back to a bench in front of the tent.

Since Finup did not answer, he continued.

"Did the emissaries upset you? I could send a party to get them back and teach them not to mess with us." The Emperor raised his hand and the general fell silent.

"No, Gampill, it is not them, it is this feeling I have been having for some time. All of this seems familiar and I do not know why. I am certain I have not been on these lands before—still the felling does not go away. I just saw myself as a child, playing in a river and at night in my dreams, I see somebody, who seems to be my father, lying dead on the ground in front of what is seems to be my home. What could this mean, Gampill? Am I losing my mind? Should we turn back and leave these people in peace, as they asked?" He stood up and started pacing up and down in front of the tent.

Another flashback made him stagger and he saw himself sitting at a table surrounded by three other men that he did not recognise. One of them looked slightly familiar though and he was the one talking, only he could not hear him. Gampill caught him again and forced him to sit down.

"My Lord, what is going on?" he asked, looking around worried to make sure nobody else noticed. "Let's go inside and rest. The long trip must have strained you to the limit. You need to lie down. Come, My Lord, let's go inside." He grabbed his arm and gently tried to get him up, but the Emperor shook his head and pulled his arm away from his grasp.

"I am all right, I don't need to rest. Gather the captains in an hour, we need to plan for the battle. Go, now. I don't need you." He stood up, turned around on his heels and entered the tent. Once inside, he fell on his knees grabbing his head in his hands, whispering.

"What is happening to me, who are these people and why do they come to me in my dreams?"

Night has fallen and Marden listened carefully, looking in the direction of the guards. They were sitting in front of the fire laughing and cheering, remembering the last battle. He shuddered at the memory of the slaughtered innocent villagers and stood up. Next to him was his friend Rotin and he leaned over to wake him up. Tonight they had to find a way to contact King Gleal and let him know they could help defeat the Emperor once and for all. They would send Brodin to take the message to him and hopefully nobody will notice him missing. After all, he was the leader of his men and he could cover up for him.

Rotin was now awake and stood up looking carefully around. Moving silently, he woke up the others and they all gathered close to their leader.

"We have to send a message to King Gleal, to let him know we are here and are waiting for his orders. Brodin, you will leave tonight with this letter. Keep it close to the river, it will take you right to the capital city. Once you cross the border, you won't need to hide, so you can go as fast as you can. You will have to find a horse though—there are villages on the way where you can ask for help and ride as fast as the horses will carry you. This is a two days journey by horse. I want you to stay with the King—do not come back alone. Give this to the King with the letter, he will understand." He took a necklace from around his neck and gave it to the young man.

"Keep it safe, the King has to get it **with** the letter."

Brodin took the letter and necklace and stashed them in his chest pocket.

"They are safe here, Master. I will go as fast as I can and give the King the message."

"The Emperor will not start preparations for the battle yet, he will wait for a week, that's what he told the emissaries, so we still have time. I hope you will get there in time so the King can prepare for the battle. The Ancestors be with you my son, hurry, it is almost time for the guards to change."

Bridon remained in the middle of the street watching the emissaries storming back to the castle. His brother had headed home but some of the other young men stayed behind and looked at each other worried. If Myrdall didn't tell them what the news was it meant that they were not bringing back good news. He turned to his father and looked at him.

"Do you think we will go to war, father? Do you think the King will call us to arms?" The old man didn't say anything, instead he looked at his neighbour Khiran and they both exchanged funny looks. As Bridon looked puzzled, the old man moved closer and spoke in a low voice.

"The Emperor will not turn back, my son, he is too arrogant to do that. He thinks he is invincible. We need to get ready. War is upon us." And with that, he turned around and headed home. He walked slowly down the street, suddenly looking older that he actually was. His son hurried to catch up with him.

"What do you mean, father? How do you know he thinks he is invincible? Have you met him before?" But the man did not answer. He only shook his head and hurried inside.

Khiran looked after him disappearing in the front yard and waved at the two men. He did not say anything either, just looked up to the sky like asking the Ancestors for advice. He turned his eyes back to the young men looking at them for answers, smiled faintly and left just like his old friend. He, too, knew that the Emperor will not turn around, but did not say how he knew that. It was not the time or place to talk about how they did.

CHAPTER 12

The Twins

The Chancellor was hurrying out of his chambers. His friend and master had sent him to meet their long lost brothers and his excitement was mixed with worry. He only had two days to get them to the palace and then they had only two more days to prepare for battle. Myrdall and Rehon were back and the news they had brought were what they had expected: the Emperor did not want to hear about turning around. Now they had to get the army ready and that will take a long time. More than they actually had. His master was worried about his son Gleal—he was away to find Gumpen, an old man that the King said would know how to defeat the Emperor and they had no news from him yet. The trip to Nill was long but he has been away for a long time and he should have send word that he is on his way back by now.

The Chief of the Guards was waiting for him in the big hall ready to leave. Brohan stopped and looked around to find his son, Myrdall and he saw him talking with the King's daughter, Llewella. He looked flushed as she was looking him in the eye. Her left hand was in his and she was smiling, looking at him fondly. Myrdall saw his father and blushed even more and moved toward him, not letting go of the girl's hand. The two walked slowly to meet him and he smiled at them.

"Father, I have asked Llewella to be my wife and she said 'yes'. I have to ask the King for her hand and I need you to be there with me." Brohan smiled again and looking at the young woman for a moment, turned to him.

"I have to go, my son, our master sent me to bring our long lost brothers home. You will have to go without me. I am sure your Father will understand milady, he knows about my trip to the borders," he said turning to the young woman. She smiled back shyly and nodded.

"Yes, Master Brohan, I know about your trip too, I have started preparations to have the guest rooms ready for them. You go and bring them home, we will go and meet Father by ourselves. Travel safely."

With a nod, she pushed Myrdall gently out of the way to make room for the soldiers that were now filling the hall, heading out to gather in the palace's yard. It was time for them to leave, if they wanted to be back on time. Brohan nodded in return and joined the Chief of the Guards. Both headed out of the door to the horses that were waiting for them. The party stormed out of the yard and Myrdall watched them go. It was time now to start preparations for the big battle.

For some time now he had this feeling that something will happen tonight during the prayer and that made him worry. He did not say anything to anybody, but as the day went on, the bad feeling was growing bigger. He went to see his father and on the way, he met his younger brother, Roban.

"Where are you going, Ropé? Are you ready for tonight? How's Tracia?" He did not wait for his brother's answer and continued.

"You look like you had that dream again. My neighbour said he had it too. It seems more people are having visions and the Elders are going to make an announcement after tonight's ceremonies. Nobody knows what they will say, but I bet there will not be good news."

Ropé sighed and looked at his brother.

"Yes, I had the *nightmare* again last night and I am getting more worried about it every day. Tracia does not need this excitement right now, she needs to get ready for the baby. I hope tonight's celebrations will bring peace to our people and we will all enjoy getting together again. Whatever the Elders will tell us, we will discuss it and then decide upon it, like we always did." He stopped not knowing what else to say. He looked worried and his brother patted him on the back, encouraging him.

"We will be all right, big brother, just trust the Ancestors. They will tell us what to do. I have to go, Rida is waiting for me to have the mid-day meal. I will see you tonight." He smiled at his brother and headed back home.

There have been three months since they left Larmar and they have been wandering around in this deserted land for days, not knowing where to go. The Elders had told them on the night of Traciana's celebrations that the Ancestors wanted them to go *back home*. They showed them where *home* was and they said that their brothers and sisters were in danger. They were the only ones who could help them and they had to hurry: time was running out for them.

They had been walking for weeks through barren land where there was nothing but hot sand or harsh rocks. They did not see any people or living creatures, just small oases spread around on their way, where they would replenish their water and gather some fruit and roots. They almost lost hope they will find the place where the Ancestors have sent them.

Today was another hot day and this time they were trying to find shelter from the burning sun in the shade of a big rugged group of rocks. They only had water and food for a few more days and Ropettian was getting more and more worried about the faith of the women and children and about the animals that were carrying the few belongings they had taken along for the journey. His wife Traciana, was due to have their baby any time now and they had to find appropriate shelter for them, away from the elements.

Lost in thought, he looked at the bright blue sky hoping for some clouds to cool them off, only to see what looked like shadows moving closer. He rubbed his tired eyes and looked up: was he starting to see things too? No, the shadows were now close enough for him to see they were white, but he could still not tell what they were. He called his brother, pointing to the sky.

"Roban, look! Do you see that?" At the sound of his voice, others started to look up, pointing to the sky. The shadows were now so close, they realised they were birds and soon they landed on the tallest rock. Seven snow white birds sitting on the hot rock—that looked surreal. Where were they coming from? Did they belong to someone?

"Where are you coming from, my little feathered friends? Is there shelter ahead? Can you lead us to it?" asked Ropettian, like he expected the birds would answer. Ignoring the man, one of the birds flew down to the ground and started picking the few bread crumbs fallen from their meal. Others joined in, cooing softly.

"They must be hungry," he heard a voice and turned to see his wife taking more bread from one of the bags lying on the ground. "They must be thirsty too," she continued, looking around for the water canteen. "Here you go, little ones, have some water. In this heat, it will make you feel better." She grabbed a metal bowl and poured some water in it, placing it next to the crumbs. The birds finished the bread and moved to the water bowl. They dipped their beaks in the water and looked around for more bread. They did not drink the water though and the woman looked at them surprised.

As she stood up to find more bread, searing pain shot in her back, making her stagger. She tried to steady herself up and hit the rock. Not able to catch her breath, she dropped down on the ground with a cry.

"Ropé, help me, the baby is coming." The man hurried to his wife and called out to a woman sitting quietly in the shade of the rock, resting, not seeing the commotion.

"Morina, the baby is coming. Bring the Sacred Readings! Hurry!"

The old woman staggered on her feet and rushed to a saddle bag on the back of a white horse and started rummaging inside. She finally found something that looked like a book wrapped in a tattered cloth. Without stopping, she called to a group of women and they came running and quickly started putting up a tent while others brought clean cloths and a rug. Another stirred the fire under an iron grate and set a big pot on it. She poured some water in it from a leather bag and went to help the others set everything up.

While the women were looking after the fire and the tent was being prepared for the birth, the men got together and started humming something that sounded like a soft lullaby. Ropettian's brother brought a torn carpet and they all sat on it under the hot sun, now singing softly.

As if they understood what was happening, the birds moved out of the way and settled back on top of the rock, waiting. After a while, soft cries of a baby came from the tent and one of the women came out and looked around to find Ropé.

"It's a girl! It's a beautiful little girl and she looks just like her mother." Smiling, she hurried back in the tent, but came back almost immediately, this time looking puzzled.

"You have another daughter, you have two daughters, master Ropé. May the Ancestors bless them and keep them safe!"

The men looked at the new father and standing up one by one, hugged him or simply shook his hand, patting him on the back. Ropé was still standing in the hot sun a little scared by the news, not knowing what to do. Morina came out of the tent again and called him.

"You can come in now, the mother is resting and you can see the babies. They are beautiful." She gently grabbed his arm, pulling him toward the tent.

Traciana was resting on the rug where she had given birth, covered by a blanket and the babies were lying next to her on the ground, wrapped up in clean cloths. He tiptoed in, carefully not to wake them up and looked at them. They were indeed beautiful and they looked just like their mother.

"I'll let them rest," he whispered to the woman. "We will have to stay here for the night. I will have the men start putting up the other tents."

He went out and saw the birds ruffling their feathers and suddenly one of them flew and landed on his shoulder. The man jumped and instinctively tried to brush it off, but it did not move. It started pecking at his hand as the others started cooing loudly. He took the bird gently off with his hand and tried to put it on the rock, but it jumped back on his shoulder. The other men stopped putting up the tents and looked at the other birds that were becoming more and more restless.

"Do you think they want to tell us something?" asked one of them. "Maybe they know a place where we can find shelter," said another one.

"The sun will start to set soon, we cannot leave now, we will get lost," said Ropé and they all turned to face him. "If the birds know of a place where we can settle, a few of us could follow them, but it is too risky to leave with the new babies without knowing where we're going. Saddle two horses and follow the birds." He turned to his brother.

"Roban, take Sandun and see where the birds will take you. We will finish setting up for the night. If you find shelter, come back and we will all leave in the morning. Travel carefully!"

Morning came and the two men were still not back. Worry filled Ropé's heart and he thought it may have not been a good idea to let them follow the birds. Nobody knew what could roam these deserted lands. He started walking out of the small camp, squinting at the horizon, hoping to see something in the distance. And then, he saw it: a cloud of dust and two dots that were moving fast, growing bigger as they were approaching the camp. As the dust cloud was getting closer, he could make out the silhouettes of the two riders that he thought lost. Two of the birds were accompanying them and this time they were carrying something in their beaks.

"You are safe!" he said rushing to help them get off the horses. "I thought you got lost. What did you find? What are the birds bringing?" Without a word, Roban dismounted and took a satchel off his saddle. He opened it and took out a handful of dried fruits and pieces of what looked like dry meat.

"There is a city not far from here, Ropé, a deserted city. I found this in one of the kitchens. Nobody has lived there for some time. The birds took us there and they showed us the place. There is food and water for us. And shelter. We need to get there before somebody else comes and claims it." Roban's eyes were filled with hope as he looked at his older brother, begging him to agree to their departure. Other men and women started to come out of the tents and joined the three men standing silently in the middle of the camp.

The birds landed on the rock and dropped their burden. They were branches of a tree they had never seen before and one of the women picked one up. It had a sweet smell and the leaves shuffled gently in the small breeze. She picked the other branches up and took them to Traciana who was just coming out of the tent. The young mother gently smoothed the leaves with her hand and tied them together with a piece of string she took out of her hair.

"We will pack up the camp and leave as soon as everybody is ready. I guess the birds will lead the way again. Or you know how to get there by yourselves?" he asked his brother. Ropettian looked around at his people and told them in a soft voice.

"Let's get ready, my friends, better times are awaiting."

Soon, the silhouettes of the white buildings started to appear in the afternoon sun. The birds were gone now and the two scouts were pointing to the city that was growing closer. The city looked deserted and some of the buildings were damaged, but most were still in good shape. *With a little bit of work we should be able to make them comfortable again*, thought Ropé. *This house would be a nice place to raise the girls and maybe have more children*, he said to himself and he stopped in front of a small house with a garden growing wildly at the front.

Then he realised they were on their way *home* and as serene as the place looked, there was no time for them to rest here for too long. They will spend the day gathering whatever food they can find and tomorrow, as soon as the sun will rise, they will be on their way again.

He looked down the narrow street that was leading to the centre of the city and he liked the lines of tall trees not known to them that were giving rich shade to the tired travellers. He stopped the wagon that carried his brand new family and told the others.

"Go around and see what you can find that will help on the way. I'll have a look at this house and see if we can stay in for the night. There should be enough places for all of us to rest. We will meet later in the centre of this city, maybe we can find out who lived here. Be careful, we don't know if this place is deserted or its people are gone only for a little while and are due to come back anytime."

CHAPTER 13

Mortoria

The land of Parmonish was renowned for its cruel ruler. General Gampill was a merciless leader and fear was all his people had known since he had taken power. For the past ten years, he had been taking over land after land in an endless war. There were no rules that he would go by in battle and he was not taking prisoners. He would only keep the men and boys that were left alive to force them fight in his army. The elderly, women and girls were of no use to him, so he would slaughter them as he would march through towns and villages.

The ones that were able to save themselves were hiding in the woods or in the mountains or were fleeing to other places seeking a safe heaven. Lately, people were running out of places for them to hide as his conquering streak was moving farther and farther away from Parmonish.

The latest battle brought him more fresh blood for his army and he was now watching his captains inspecting the men they had just captured. Sitting in front of his tent, wrapped up in furs to keep him warm on that chilly morning, he looked around the camp at the people running about. Some were tending to the wounded, others were bringing over groups of young men tied together, pulling them out of large chuck wagons lined around the camp to be inspected. Many others were just sitting in front of big campfires eating or drinking or simply resting after the battle.

Their exhausted faces were covered in blood and mud. He had lost a lot of good people during this last battle—the enemy had put up a hell of a fight and at one point he thought he would have to pull back. But the experience of his army and the numbers had finally given them the advantage and he managed to push them back inside the city walls. Some of the enemy soldiers were cut off from their comrades and he had them now at his mercy.

The sun was rising and the sky was red in the east. His eyes stopped as he caught something at the horizon. He asked for his spyglass and looked again towards the west, where he could see a huge cloud of dust closing in. He shouted at one of the soldiers who was standing guard and he came running.

"What is that getting closer?" he shouted, pointing away from the camp. "Send the guards to investigate!" he growled as the soldier run away, bowing. A group of soldiers who had been sitting around a camp fire drinking hot drinks close to his tent, jumped up and started running to their horses. Their leader came out of a tent nearby and mounting, led the group away.

As the scouts were moving farther away, the general stood up and a soldier rushed to catch the fur blankets before they touched the ground. From behind the tent, another came quickly and whispered something in the general's ear. The General turned to the man and raised his hand ready to hit him with his gloved hand, but the man fell to the ground on his knees begging for forgiveness.

"Bring him to me, now!" he bellowed and the man struggled back on his feet, rushing back to where he came from. Almost instantly he returned with an old man guarded by two armoured soldiers who pushed him toward the General. The man stumbled and fell to the ground, only to be grabbed again by the soldiers that pulled him back on his feet. His tied up feet prevented him from walking fast and that angered Gampill. He pulled the old man closer to him and holding him by his ripped clothes, he snarled in his face.

"You though you can get away from me, old man? I have not kept you alive to cause trouble, but because we need information and you are going to give it to us, whether you want it or not!" He let go of the clothes and the man struggled to keep his balance. His hands were bound at the front with thick rope and the wrists were blue from the tightness.

Unexpectedly, he raised his bound hands and tried to hit the General, but the soldiers caught him just as the fists swiped his cheek and pushed him to the ground.

"I would rather die than tell you anything, you monster!" he shouted as the soldiers started kicking him. "There is nothing I have to say to you. Only that I wish I was dead before you could shame me like this!" The soldiers kept kicking the man, shouting and swearing at him, but the General stopped them and knelled down next to him. Grabbing him by the hair, he shouted in his face.

"I *may* be a monster and you may *wish* you were dead, but you are not, and my men *will* make you talk, Mortor. Bring her!" he shouted as he turned to an older soldier who had been standing back, watching.

"Bring her here and we will see if he has anything to tell us". The old man looked up furiously and cried.

"No, leave her alone, she doesn't know anything."

The city of Mortoria was steadily growing larger and people had to find new land to build their homes on. During the past years, lots of people moved here from other parts of the world to make this quiet and prosperous city their home. The Elders welcomed everybody and they all shared in the wealth the earth had to offer. The city was flanked by two large rivers that provided water for people and beasts. The forest not far from the city, gave them the wood to build their homes and the fields were large enough for them to grow crops to feed everybody.

Word of the riches of Mortoria was spreading and with that, thoughts of envy and greed had started to threaten its people. Lately, strangers started coming in the city scouting around and that made some of the locals nervous. Then, flocks of women with young children and older folks started to arrive asking for sanctuary. They carried only a few bundles with personal belongings and their frightened looks made everybody feel uneasy. They were telling stories about war and how they had been forced to flee their homes. They were praising the Ancestors for their luck to be alive and cursed the monster who had taken their lands and homes and their men away from their families.

The last group to come to the city was smaller and the few people, mostly young women, guarded by a dozen soldiers, looked different than the others that had arrived in the City. They were riding well groomed horses and were accompanied by a few large wagons guarded by more armed men. It was the first group to bring their own tents and food and water and they headed straight to the city center, asking to meet with their Elders. The young woman that seemed to be their leader was dressed in simple robes, but the determination on her face made her stand out from the others. Her long hair was carefully tied up and around her neck a delicate golden chain held a pendant that looked like a bird.

"My name is Johanna, daughter of Torban and I would like to talk to your council. There are urgent matters I need to tell them about and there is little time," she told the people who met her as she and her party approached the city center. She stopped in front of a group of people talking in the small plaza, asking them for help, when a young woman came out of a large building that seemed to be the meeting place of the City Council. She invited the young woman inside while the onlookers followed her but stopped at the entrance. She waived at her people to wait for her and rushed to catch up with her guide.

The two women entered the council house and headed for a small door at the end of the hall. The room had a tall arched ceiling covered by beautiful paintings showing people going about their daily lives, children playing and crops ready to be harvested. The bright colours made the walls friendly and the light filtered by the arched windows gave a warm tint to the peoples' faces. There were several doors in the hallway but the young woman headed straight for the one right across the main entrance and stopped in front of it. She knocked gently and a strong voice asked her to come in.

As the door opened, the woman stepped back and invited her guest in. Johanna entered and the door closed behind her. A middle aged man stood up and came to greet her. The room was just as warm as the hallway and the woman felt comfortable as he approached her.

"I am Mortor, the head of the council and leader of the city of Mortoria. Please come in. We were told you were bringing important news and that you needed to talk to us. These are the other council members and we are ready to listen to you." Six other people, four men and two women sitting around a horseshoe shaped table, smiled and nodded at their guest.

"Please, have a seat and tell us what brings you to Mortoria."

"There is no time to waste, Master Mortor, war is upon us. I am here to warn you about General Gampill's army heading your way. You have to get ready to fight him and I can help you defeat him." Silence fell in the room and as soon as she finished delivering the news, the woman sat down with a big tired sigh.

The three men stopped on the side of the road to rest. It was hot and not a cloud in the sky to protect them from the heat. The tall trees they have finally gotten to, were giving a rich shade and they dropped on the ground exhausted. They only had food and water for one more day and if they could not find shelter soon they would have no chances of survival in this deserted land. One of the men opened his satchel and took out a piece of dry bread and a canteen of water. He broke it in three and handed a piece to each of his friends. Silently, they chewed the food and tried to find shade from the burning sun closer to the trunk of one tree. The man who seemed to be their leader, looked at the sky and then at his companions.

"We need to find a place to settle for the night and I guess here, between these trees we can build a fire and sleep over night." The other two looked at him and then away.

"We should have found the city by now," the younger one started and stopped suddenly. Fear shined in his eyes and he took the canteen from the ground and pretended to drink. The older man threw him a fierce look and stood up.

"I wanted what was best for us, Rotin. When we decided to leave Saranda, we decided it together. I did not force you to come with me, you **wanted** to come. And now, your complaining and whining is not going to take us anywhere. We need to keep going and we will find the city, but we need to have faith." He stopped in front of the young man, crouched down and looking him in the eye snarled.

"If you do not want to continue your journey with us, you are free to go back. Nobody is keeping you here." He took a few steps squinting toward the west, hoping that when the sun will set, the heat will let up. Then, he saw something in the distance and turned to the others.

"Look, someone is coming. Look there!" he shouted excited. The other two stood up quickly and looked where he was pointing. A cloud of dust was getting closer and they quickly grabbed their belongings.

Soon, a group of riders arrived and their leader pulled the reigns to stop the horse. His companions stopped their horses too and all dismounted swiftly.

"Good day, strangers and may the Ancestors keep you safe! What are you doing alone in this deserted place and where are you headed?" he asked the strangers. The leader of the group moved closer and with a bow answered.

"I am Finup and these are my friends Marden and Rotin. We have been travelling for a long time and are looking for the city of Mortoria. Do you know where it is?" The strangers looked at each other and smiled. Finup continued.

"We want to settle there and the people in Saranda told us that there is work for us to earn our living. We will also need shelter for tonight and some food and water." He stopped to see if the man believed him and as he saw the reluctant look on his face, added quickly.

"We can pay for it. If you tell us where the city is, we will be on our way."

The rider looked at his companions as if to ask for their approval, but then he chuckled and stepped closer to Finup extending his hand.

"Of course we know where Moratoria is, we are heading there too. And yes, there is lots of work for anybody who wants to work and also plenty of food and water. You are more than welcome to be our guests as long as you want to." Shaking their hands, he continued.

"Mortoria is not far from here. You cannot see it yet because of the hills in the distance, but as soon as you pass that line of trees you should be able to see the first houses. Come to the centre of the city and look for the inn. Tell them you talked to Mortor and they will give you rooms to rest and food to eat. Come and see me tomorrow at the Council Hall," he finished as he mounted his horse.

His party got on their horses too and with a quick wave they continued east. A cloud of dust followed them and the three men stood there for a few minutes, dazzled. Marden was the first to pull himself together and grabbing his satchel, started running after the riders. The others followed him and ignoring the heat, tried to keep up.

Mortoria was a nice place to live, nicer than the others where the "strangers" had lived before. Even the old houses were well maintained, the gardens were little oases of green vegetation. People were friendly and they had greeted them and offered them food and board without asking for anything in return. Rotin was thinking that he would want to settle here. He wanted to get married and start a family and this seemed the perfect place for that. His friend Marden was building a house to take his new bride into and that made him feel too, that this was the end of his journey.

Only Finup was always thinking of going away and he did not understand why—the Mortorians had greeted them with friendship and allowed them to stay for as long as they wanted. Soon after they arrived, they offered to help them find work around the city and get a place to stay. He had met a young woman about a year ago and he wished he could find the courage to go and ask for her hand. Her father was a very strict man and he was afraid he would turn him down. Orana was a smart and beautiful young woman and her family was one of the wealthiest in the city. He did not have much, only what he could gather by working here and there in the past years. He could not offer her much, but she liked him too and he hoped that she would accept him as her husband.

It's been seven years since he arrived in Mortoria with his two companions and his status in the city has changed. His friends had been looking for simple, earthly things, like getting married or building a house, but his expectations were much higher than that. People were looking up to him and respected him although he was not a *local*. Two years ago, people elected him to be their representative in the City Council and that made him very proud. He knew he could one day become the leader of the city but for now he was one of the Elders and his word was worth something. In spite of that, lately he felt he could do more than just listen to Mortor tell him what to do. He felt that his role in the city council should change and when he had heard about this *ring*, an heirloom that was the city's protector, he tried to find out more. He also heard that the person who would hold it had special powers and would be one of the most respected people in Mortoria.

It was late at night and he woke up from the dream he has been having for some time now. In his dream, the emerald ring on his finger made him feel confident and invincible. He realised that whatever powers of the ring had, transferred to him when he had placed it on. He decided to take it off but then he changed his mind. He did not want that soothing feeling to go away, so he left it on.

The man stood up and went to the window. He could see the City Council building with the light of the street lanterns shining over it. He had to do something about that ring and maybe tomorrow, when the council would be in session again, he could persuade Mortor to vote on who the new Ring Bearer should be. He knew that many of the councillors would support him and maybe he could turn some of the undecided ones in his favour. He had until the morning to find the way and, as he was getting dressed, his mind was fervently thinking about how to do that.

"My Lord Mortor, we need to decide on who the new Ring Bearer will be," Councillor Chartor said, standing up. "It is time for its power to be put to work. I vote for Councillor Finup," he said, turning toward his protégé smiling. "He is a wise man and has been looking after the welfare of our city since he came here seven years ago. I trust him with my life and I know people respect and trust him too. I say we vote for it." Murmurs rose in the room and Mortor stood up asking for everybody's attention.

"I agree, Master Chartor, we should decide who the new Ring Bearer is. I too, trust Finup and I think he is the right person for this important job. But, today we have more important issues to discuss."

He stopped and sat down.

"Word of a general conquering lands and killing people has come to my attention. Lately, some of our people came to me to say that strangers arrived in the city, spying around, looking for weaknesses in the city's defences. They have been going around asking questions about our army and if there is anything special that keeps our city safe from invaders. It worries me to learn about that and we need to make sure none of these strangers find out about our defences. They cannot know about the Ring and its power."

"Master Mortor, I suggest we build a wall around the city to keep the enemies away. The powers of the Ring alone may not be enough to keep us safe."

Mortor looked up to see who was talking. "There is no time for that, brother Finup. We need to find out what can help us protect our people *right now.*" He smiled and continued.

"I find this idea to be a great one but we do not have time to build a wall. We need to contact our neighbours and let them know danger is coming. We could have riders ready to go to them for help in case we need it." Finup stood up and looked him in the eye.

"Our neighbours may not be able to come to our rescue in time, Master Mortor, we need to look after ourselves for as long as we can before others can give us help. I say the wall would offer better protection and if we start now, we should be able to finish it before winter comes." Some of the other Councillors nodded in agreement, while others argued there was no time for that.

Mortor stood up again and asked for them to settle down and spoke once more.

"We can vote on this and then talk to our people and ask for their opinion. What the people will decide, that is what we will do. Who is for building a protective wall around the city?" Five people stood up and voted in favour of the wall. The other two, including Mortor, voted against it.

"The people have spoken," he said. "We will now go talk to our people and ask about the wall. We shall come back in a week to report our findings and whatever they may be, we will take it. May the Ancestors keep you safe!"

CHAPTER 14

The Ring

The sun was rising over the field covered by strewn bodies. Horses were grazing around not bothered by the smell of the blood filling the air and birds were chirping calling out to their mates. The tall man stood on his horse and looked at the bodies covered in blood and mud and sighed.

"What a waste of young life," he said to himself. And what made it sadder was that it all happened because of treason. His army would have pushed General Gampill's army back until help arrived. But now, here they were in this field, gathering their dead and most likely preparing for surrender. They would have not been defeated if it wasn't for the traitor Finup.

He had sided with their enemy and turned against his people. He was the holder of the Sacred Ring—he had been elected by the council members to be the Ring Bearer just a couple of years ago and they had trusted him with their lives. For now, their families were safe, but as long as he had the Ring, he could finish them as easily as squishing an ant under his foot. The truce they agreed upon allowed them to gather their dead and hopefully any wounded and now that they were on the field, seeing the bodies lying on the ground brought rage and desperation in his heart: why did this happen to them?

A few years ago, they had welcomed Finup and his friends with open arms and gave them all they needed to help them start a new life. They helped them build homes and now they all had families and were a happy part of their community. After a while, people appointed Finup to the city council: he was a smart man, with bright ideas about their future and the one who came up with the idea of building the protective walls around the city. Nobody liked the idea at the time and some opposed it, thinking there were no dangers Mortoria needed protection from, but now, everybody was thankful for it. Unfortunately, none of that mattered now, the city had been defeated and the only hope to save it was to get the Ring back. Johanna, the young woman who warned them of the coming of General Gampill's army, managed to escape and she promised she will do anything to take the Ring back even if it meant to give her life for it.

He turned towards the young men that accompanied them and dismounted. They joined him and started to gather the dead and load them into the carts. There were no survivors, and as the General was not taking prisoners, it appeared that the wounded had been slaughtered, too. The able bodied were taken to become soldiers in his army and maybe fight against their brothers and fathers. The carts filled quickly and Mortor gestured to his companions to head back to the city. He would stay behind with a handful of people to look for any survivors.

As the carts were slowly moving away, he kneeled and started praying for the souls of the dead. Lost in prayer, he did not hear the people sneaking behind him. Suddenly one of his men shouted something, but he heard his voice like in a dream and as he turned to see what he was saying, he could only see the sword raised over his head and everything turned black.

He woke up to find himself bound and lying on the ground in a tent that reeked of blood and sweat. He tried to sit up, but the binds on his arms and legs kept him from doing that. He tried kneeling and he finally managed to get up struggling, trying to steady himself. The flap to the tent was open and he couldn't see anybody watching it. Carefully, he stepped over the bodies of people he did not know—he could not tell if they were dead or alive—and spied outside to check if it was safe for him to get out. He wondered where his men were—were they here or have they been slaughtered on the battle field as he was being kidnapped? Right at that moment a soldier showed in the doorway and they both stopped, starring at each other. The soldier realised what he was trying to do and hit him in the chest the blow making him fall on his knees. The soldier quickly grabbed him by his coat and pulled him up.

"Where do you think you're going, old man," he growled. He called to another man sitting on a low stool cleaning his weapon. "Hey, Bartan, tell the General the prisoner is awake and he wanted to escape. Go now!" he growled as he saw the man was not moving fast enough. *Bartan* stood up and rushed away only to return after a few moments.

"The General wants to talk to the prisoner. Bring him over!" They both grabbed the man by his armpits and dragged him toward a big tent sitting in the middle of the camp. They dropped him on the ground in front of an armoured man.

Johanna was now getting closer to the enemy camp and stopped to look through her spyglass, to locate the General's tent. She signalled to her three companions to wait for her as she moved closer. The sun was setting and she could not see too far, but the flag on top of a tall tent was standing out in the dim light and she looked back at her companions to let them know she was going alone. The oldest of the three men quickly moved closer to her and whispered.

"Milady, you cannot go by yourself. You need our help. Please let us come with you." The young woman shook her head and grabbing his arm spoke to him in a soft voice.

"I have to go alone, Marden, you go back to the city and have everybody ready to leave. I will try to get the Ring back and if I do, I will join you as soon as I can, but we have to save what is left of Mortoria. Help will not come in time and we cannot sacrifice peoples' lives in vain. Nobody can defeat him alone and now, with the power of the Ring, he is even stronger." She stopped and looked fondly at the man and hugged him.

"Go quickly and may the Ancestors be with you! Save our brothers and sisters and send word to the neighbours that their help cannot stop the invasion and they must prepare to leave at a moment's notice. If I am not back by morning, get everybody ready and leave."

She turned around and started walking quickly toward the camp. She hoped the dark will conceal her and she would be able to enter the camp without being seen. The three men watched her for a while and then turned back to the city. There was no time to lose and they started to run quietly in the cool night.

The camp was quiet now and the young woman tried to guess where Gampill's tent would be. Most of the men were sleeping on blankets placed directly on the ground and a guard was watching over them. The tents were lit and voices could be heard from within. Nobody was guarding them and she sneaked quietly between them, listening for any movement. She finally found it in the middle of the camp and stopped. Two guards were pacing up and down in front of the door and she counted how long it took them to go from one side to the other . . . . three, four, five, six, seven . . . eleven paces and then they turned around and there were eleven more paces in the opposite direction. There were only a few moments when the soldiers were too far apart to hear each other and that was her chance of moving closer to the tent, maybe to try to get in.

She was taking a big chance doing that, but she had to. She had to find out where Finup was and get the Ring back, otherwise the fate of Mortoria was sealed, and with that, their neighbours' as well. She waited until the soldiers were at the end of their route and moved closer to the tent. The full moon did not help her, it was shining brightly and it showed all the details on the ground. She counted again and came out from behind a wagon parked by the tent. Looking at the two soldiers, she sneaked over quietly and entered. She managed to make it inside without being seen! The tent had a small antechamber and luckily nobody was there. She listened carefully and heard two men talking softly. She thought she heard Finup's voice but she could not make out what he was saying. Moving closer to the entrance of the other room, she could now hear him.

"We need to use the Ring to take down Mortoria. If they manage to take it back, we will never be able to go farther into the land. Gampill, we already have Mortor. We need to find the young woman who warned them about your coming. She knows about its powers and she needs to be stopped too." The other voice that she recognised as the General's, answered back.

"You trust too much the power of this Ring, Finup. I did not need a *ring* to get where I am now," he mocked him. "I only had my army and my men and that was enough." She could sense he was growing annoyed by the other man's insistence on using the Ring and hope filled her heart. Maybe he will send Finup away and she would be able to retrieve it and give it back to its rightful owner.

But as she was preparing to leave the tent, something strange happened. A bright light shone through the cloth and she heard a booming voice talking. It seemed to be Finup's, but she could not be certain. It sounded strange and non-human and suddenly she heard screams coming from inside.

"You should not doubt the power of the Ring, General," the voice said. "I will show you its powers," the voice said and the screaming continued. The General's voice was begging for mercy and as quickly as the light started, as quickly it stopped. Johanna looked around, worried that the guards may have heard the screaming and looked for a place to hide, in case they would show up. But nobody came in and she let out a big sigh of relief. Besides, there was nowhere for her to hide anyway—the antechamber was empty.

There was nothing else for her to do in there, so she decided to leave. Finup had shown the General the power of the Ring and he probably has him under his control now. She had to return to Mortoria and tell the others about that, as quickly as she could. There was really nothing they could do now and their only hope was to join forces with others to try to keep Finup, and the General, from taking over the City until they could find a way of getting the Ring back.

She turned to leave, when suddenly, the flap of the main room pulled open and Finup saw her. Without hesitation he grabbed her by her robes and pulled her toward her.

"What are you doing here, Johanna, are you spying on me?" he growled pulling her close to him. The woman struggled to free herself, but the man was stronger. He did let go though, and she whimpered as that made her lose her balance. Right then, Gampill came out and when he saw her, froze. It took only a moment though to pull himself together and with a savage look in his eyes, hollered for the guards. Still on the ground, Johanna struggled to get back on her feet, but the guards arrived and grabbing her, pulled her up.

"Take her and put her with the others," Gampill shouted to the two soldiers. "You have all night to think about whose side you want to join, *Milady*," he mocked her. "My advice is our side is better, but it is up to you. If you want to live, you will want to join the winning party." As they were taking her away, the woman shouted back.

"I will never join you, you murderers, not even if you kill me. I would rather die than live my live as a traitor."

CHAPTER 15

True Heirs

The King sat back in front of the book and continued reading. His last experience has been frightening and he understood now that he had to read every page in the Book if he wanted to really understand how it all came to happen and how to deal with the danger that the Emperor was posing to his family and people.

His son was on his way back to the palace with an old man whom he knew nothing about. The Spirit told him that his presence was essential if they wanted to turn the balance of the forces in their favour. His Councillor was meeting the descendants of the Bird people and they too would help defeat the evil. Now it was his turn to find out what else they needed to stop the Emperor and reset everything in order.

The next chapter in the book was named "True Heirs" and that got his attention. Who were the *true heirs* and where were they?

Long ago, when the last direct descendant of the King Bird went to join the Ancestors, the throne was inherited by Nill, his great-nephew. King Rondal and his wife, Queen Minada didn't have any children so they decided to adopt. They were not getting any younger and while they were still in good health, it was time for them to find an heir to the throne. There were lots of things the boy would have to learn: the court life was quite intricate and the laws had to be followed quite strictly.

The Queen's older brother had two sons and one daughter and they had children of their own. One summer, during the Roses Festival, the King invited them to the palace and that is when they met Nill. He was his niece's eldest son. He was only 10 at the time and maybe too young to become the heir of such a large kingdom, but the young boy was so impressed with the court life that he asked his parents to let him stay at the palace after the family returned home. He wanted to learn about his Ancestors and where they came from. After a while, the Queen asked the boy if he wanted to stay at the palace forever. They would of course talk to his parents and ask for their permission, but if he wanted, in time he would learn everything about the kingdom and become their heir.

Nill's parents were saddened about their son's decision but they allowed him to stay. Eventually, Nill became part of the King Rondal's family and his training as the King's heir started. The young boy took his responsibilities very seriously in spite of his young age and when he turned thirty, his father retired and left him in charge. They had taught young Nill everything he needed to know about how to rule the kingdom and about their traditions, so he was ready.

Five years after his coronation, Nill met Ronda, a beautiful young woman from Gardal, a land far away and he decided to marry her. They had met during the Harvest Festival when her family came to celebrate the crops and they fell in love. Soon after, they got married and Ronda moved to the City of Bridd. King Nill and his wife had four children, two sons and a pair of twins: a daughter and a son. Their life was quiet and happy and when their eldest son, Nill Sunden came of age, they both retired and left the big city just like his adoptive parents. They wanted to find a place where they could enjoy their old age without the burden of the court duties and found a piece of land close to a forest and crossed by a large river. They named the place Nill and built their home there. In time, people started to come and settle nearby and that is how the village of Nill was established.

Years have passed and they were living happily surrounded by their grandchildren and villagers. One day, without any warning, the Queen fell ill and soon after went to the Ancestors. Saddened by her sudden passing, King Nill built a shrine, not far from their home to help him and others remember his wife by. In time, people started to build homes around it and they named the village "Ronda", in her memory.

King Nill's eldest son and heir, Sunden was a kind King and his people respected him for his wisdom and the way he ruled the *kingdom. His two younger brothers looked up to him too. Life was peaceful, just like before and somewhat uneventful, so King Nill's two younger sons decided to leave the kingdom to find what they called "adventures". Their sister, Norria mocked them that they were getting too old for this, but they laughed back and started preparations for their departure.*

Soon after their mother's passing, Norria had moved to Nill, to look after their father. He was getting older and the loss of his beloved wife had weakened his heart. One rainy fall morning, old King Nill sent word for his sons. He felt his time had come and he had some important matters to tell them about before he went to join his wife and the Ancestors. His daughter was with him when her brothers arrived and they all entered the large sunroom to talk.

King Nill had a chest in his lap and showed his children to the chairs arranged around the room. They all sat down and he started with a shaky voice. "Long ago, there were three brothers who inherited four magical gifts from their father. They were passed on from generation to generation and just like my father inherited them from his, I got them from my father. It is time you learn about them and why they are so important to us and our people."

He took the chest from his lap and placed it on the small table next to him. He opened it with shaking hands and took out a bundle. Unwrapping the cloth, he revealed two identical necklaces, a dagger and a gem. The old man took one of the necklaces in his hands and fondly looked at it.

"This was your mother's," he said looking at Norria. "It is yours now." He gave her the necklace and the young woman put it around her neck. The King smiled—she reminded him of his wife and thought that the necklace looked perfectly on her.

He then turned to his eldest son and took the dagger out of the bundle.

"This is the Royal Dagger, Sunden, look after it carefully as it has great powers." The young man took it gently from his father's hands and looked at it. Its hilt was covered by four diamonds that surrounded a ruby placed in their middle. With identical designs on both sides, the precious stones were making a cross and that made it look like a holy heirloom, not a weapon.

"This is the Wisdom Stone, a gem that has magical powers and keeps people fair and straight," he turned toward his youngest son. *"Look after it with care, my son. He who has it, will be able to find the answer in the most difficult of situations. It belonged to your great-uncle and he was known to be a very wise man."*

He then turned to his middle son and took the second necklace.

"You are my second son and your sister's twin brother, so you will get the second necklace, the twin of your sister's. They both talk to each other and you will each know when your twin sibling needs your help." He turned to his daughter and smiled.

"You will know when Dorden needs you. Your necklace will turn red and the stones will fade."

"This is my inheritance to you all, look after them with care, nobody can know about them. Without them, you are just regular people. With them, you will have the power to stop evil and restore peace."

The sun was setting and Ropettian was sitting on the bench at the front of his house. There have been two years since they left Larmar and the "visions" stopped. He did not know what that meant. Did that mean that they had finally arrived *home*? But in his visions, the land had rivers and fields, not rugged mountains and fast rivers. His brother thought that maybe they *were* home—after all if the visions stopped, they had no way of knowing where to go next. But Ropé didn't think so. He and some of the others who joined them those years ago said that although the visions stopped there was something that told them this was not the end of their journey. The birds that led them to this place had left soon after they arrived in this deserted city.

A few days after their arrival they started looking around to learn more about this place. They had found what looked like council chambers and inside there was a room filled with parchments and books. They had divided them amongst themselves hoping they will find out what this city had been, its name, maybe the name of the people who lived here.

So far, they had learned that the place was called *Mortoria* and its leaders were descendants of Toran Mordon who settled here and build the place. They have found some drawings showing the borders and who their neighbours were; there were deeds of places with names of people who owned them; birth and marriage papers arranged by date and many other documents, but nothing to tell them where these people had gone.

After a while, they got tired of reading them and were about to abandon this daunting task, when they came upon a locked room hidden by a huge portrait of probably one of the city's leaders. They came to find it by mistake: one of the people trying to move a few chairs out of the way to get to another shelf of parchments, had tripped over a loose board in the floor and leaned on the picture. It had moved and revealed the vault. They had been looking for a key to the room for some time but they had not been able to find it. They tried to force it open but that did not work either—the door was made of some sort of material they couldn't break or burn. They had decided to leave it for now and look around in the other rooms, maybe the key was in one of them.

He was lost in thought, when he heard his daughters coming down the road, running with their mother following behind. They had been down the street to visit their friends and the girls were now chasing each other laughing. He stood up to meet them and grabbing them both in his arms, smiled and gave them a cuddly hug. The girls giggled and wriggled out of his arms, so he put them down. Their mother caught up with them and smiled fondly at him.

"Hello, there, stranger," she greeted him. "How has your day been?" He smiled back at her and answered.

"Not as good as yours, I see. How are Fronda and the children?"

The woman sat down on the bench and Ropé sat down beside her putting his arm around her.

"They are all right, Fronda cooked some of her special desserts and the girls had a lot of fun with their friends. How has your day been, you are lost in thought again. Is everything all right?" He looked over to where the girls were playing and answered.

"We still couldn't find the key to the vault and I believe that room holds the answer to the mystery of this city. We still have a lot of rooms to search and that takes time."

Suddenly, one of the girls shrieked and he turned to see what had happened. A hole had opened in the ground and she had fallen in there. Tracia rushed to her daughter and grabbed her by the hands pulling her gently up. The girl was scared but unharmed and she started crying softly. Ropettian followed in his wife's footsteps and stopped surprised on the edge of the small pit. Then he smiled and crouched down to look at something at its bottom.

As he lifted the small wooden box, he saw a bird engraved on it and put it down on the ground. He had a feeling that the box held the answer to their questions and he took it inside. He didn't want to open it yet, so he put it on the table and looked at it. Excitement and an uneasy feeling made his heart jump and he decided to leave it there and go look for his brother. They should open the box together and he told Tracia that he has to go get him. She looked alarmed at her husband—she had never seen him so worried and also excited and got the girls inside.

"What is the matter, Ropé, what did you find?" He did not answer and left the room quickly. This discovery could be the answers to why the visions stopped—he had a funny feeling about it and he needed to get the others to see it too.

CHAPTER 16

Old Man Gumpen

"Frona, go and tell the boys to saddle the horses," the inn keeper called to his wife. "I am taking His Lordship to Master Gumpen." He turned to Gleal and continued.

"My Lord, I will take you to his house. He cannot walk, he has been ailing for many years now, but maybe when he will hear that the kingdom needs him, his strength will return to his body."

The man grabbed his hat and coat and headed toward the door, Gleal and his companions following. A path formed in the inn and everybody was now standing and respectfully bowed as the young messengers were leaving he room.

Outside, the horses were ready and they all mounted and spurred them in haste. The innkeeper was leading the way and the gallop of the hooves covered the whistling wind. Snow started to fall lightly and the travellers wrapped their bodies in their cloaks trying to keep themselves warm.

The small neat houses of Nill started to appear in the haze and Randan pulled the reins. The others caught up with him and slowed down. Gleal looked at him and he pointed to a small house with a neatly cut hedge.

"That is where Gumpen lives, My Lord," he said. "He lives there with his wife Rubana. Their children are now married and have left them, so they are all alone. People go and help them from time to time, because their eldest son, Finup, who should have been their help, passed away many years ago and they have nobody to look after them." Sadness filled his voice and he turned his horse heading for the house. The snow had stopped but the wind was whipping their faces and they hurried to get inside, in the warm house.

Gleal dismounted and walked slowly toward the door. He knocked gently and they heard movement inside. A kind voice called.

"Who goes there in this weather?" The door opened suddenly and an old woman wrapped in a woollen shall, stared, a little scared, but also surprised at the young man. Then she saw Randan and smiled.

"What brings you here, Randan?" she started. Then she looked again at the three strangers and asked them smiling.

"Are you friends of Randan's?" The innkeeper stepped closer to the door and turning to Gleal to ask for permission to speak, smiled back at the woman.

"They are messengers from the Big City, Mother Rubana. They bring news and they need to talk to Master Gumpen."

The woman jumped at the words "Big City" and looked again at Gleal. She stepped aside to let them enter as if she suddenly recognised them and the four men stomped their feet on the threshold to shake the snow off and took their hats off in respect. Inside, the smell of fresh baked bread and the warmth coming from the stove in the corner of the room surrounded them and for a moment the tired travellers forgot about their mission. But then they heard a voice coming through an open door.

"Who's there Ruba? Is that Randan that I hear?" Randan got closer to the door and spoke to the man.

"Yes, that is me, Master Gumpen. I bring some messengers from the Big City. They travelled here to talk to you on behalf of the King."

Silence filled the room and Gleal stepped forward. Bowing respectfully, he addressed Rubana who was now standing in front of the stove crumpling a cloth in her hands, not knowing what to do.

"My name is Gleal, mother Rubana, I am the son of King Lade-Gleal and I come to your house for help. I must talk to Master Gumpen, I have a message for him from my father and with his help we can defeat the Emperor."

The shock of Gleal's words was too much for the old woman. She tried to move towards a chair by the window but she tripped over the leg of the stove and Gleal caught her and steadied her on the feet. Embarrassed by her clumsiness, the woman finally found the strength to walk to a chair nearby and fell in it still holding the cloth.

The sound of footsteps came from the other room and an old man appeared in the doorway. He stopped and leaned on a cane, then slowly turned and looked at Gleal. The young man rummaged through a satchel under his coat and took a small package out. Then he rummaged again inside and took out a letter bearing the King's seal. He moved toward the old man and handed him the package and the letter. Gumpen took it and slowly, with shaking steps he headed toward a small bench and sat down. He unwrapped it and looked inside.

Shock and surprise filled his face and looked at his wife who jumped at the sight of its contents. He then turned toward Gleal and asked with shaking voice.

"Where did you get this My Lord? I thought it was lost 15 years ago when my eldest son Finup left us."

A new day started and Rubana went out to fetch water from the village fountain. Today, like all days since her eldest son left, she started her day fetching water, hoping to see him coming back. But day after day passed and he did not return so she felt more heartbroken every time she would return home alone. She filled her bucket and slowly headed back, thinking that Finup was probably dead and his body buried in some strange land without a tomb stone to tell who he was. She was trudging home with the water, when the sound of hooves made her stop. She moved out of the way and put her load down on the side of the road. As she turned to see who was coming, was surprised to see a strange man in a cart pulled by a pair of mules. The old woman stood there waiting for the cart to pass, but the man pulled the reins and the mules stopped. He smiled at her and tipped his hat.

"Good day, Mother Rubana and may the Ancestors keep you safe!" The woman's heart jumped and she tried to grab the bucket and hurry on her way, but the man jumped down from the cart and getting closer, continued.

"You do not know me Mother, but I know you and I have news about your son, Finup. My name is Gardal, son of Rogashan and I come from Ronda."

The woman stopped and looked at the man once again. She knew Rogashan, he was one of the Elders of Ronda, but she did not know any of his sons.

"You say you are Rogashan's son?" The man nodded and smiled again and she continued. "What brings you here and why are you upsetting me by telling me you have news of my son? He is long gone and maybe buried in some strange land, forgotten by everybody." Tears choked her and she tried to grab the bucket again to get on her way, but the young man was faster and grabbed it for her.

"I will carry this for you, Mother, if you would let me. I need to talk to you and Master Gumpen. I need to talk to the other parents that lost their sons and daughters when they left Nill." He looked her in the eye as he talked, so she let him carry the bucket. The two started walking side by side, with the mules following behind and the man continued.

"My brother left too, you know, and my mother died of broken heart because of that. I was very young when he went away, I do not remember him. My father swore to find him and bring him back and he did find him, but he does not want to come back. He and his friends are now living in the Big City and the lure of new life keeps them there, away from their families."

The woman stopped and stared at the ground.

"He broke my heart, too, Gardal. One morning he was gone and we looked everywhere and asked everybody, but no one knew where they went, so we gave up and moved on. Life has not been the same since, but we have to go on. We still work the land; the carts are still loaded for the Harvest Festival. People still get married and have children—life *has* to go on," she whispered.

She looked at the man and pointed. "We are here. I will go get my husband." Grabbing the bucket, she opened the gate and entered the front yard. She left the gate open for the young man to follow her, but he stopped respectfully.

The woman left the bucket on the front steps and went inside. Shortly after, an old man came out and gestured him to a bench under a tree to the side of the house. The two sat down and said nothing for a while. Then, the old man finally started, looking away.

"What do you know about my son, Gardal? Where is he? Have you seen him?" Without answering, the man stood up and went to his cart. He returned with a bundle and put it on the bench next to the old man, sitting down. Gumpen looked at him inquisitively and the young man untied it. In it, there were a few pieces of paper and he grabbed one of them.

He looked at it, like he wanted to make sure it was the right one, and passed it on. The paper looked new and when the old man unfolded it, he gasped. His hands started to shake and he called for his wife. She came quickly—he could tell she had been waiting somewhere close—and the man showed her the paper. Tears came into her eyes and she covered her mouth. He moved to make room for her to sit, but the young man stood up in respect and moved away to give them some space.

Looking at his wife, he started reading. "Dear Mother and Father. I hope this letter finds you well. I am now living in the Big City and life is good . . ."

Quietly, Gardal took his bundle and returned to his cart. He got in and called out to the mules who started walking slowly, the sound of their hooves covering Gumpen's words. His next stop would be at Romdan's house. He had a letter from their daughter and he hoped to find them well.

The trip to the Big City had been long and the old man was tired, but here he was, looking for his son. He got word that his son was living at the palace and he was heading there, maybe somebody could help him. He stopped to look around and he saw the clean streets and the beautiful gardens and understood why people all over the land came to the Big City: it gave you a feeling of security and made you proud of living in such a great place.

The palace was just ahead and he hurried to get there. He stopped at the gate and asked for his son. A guard told him to wait and returned shortly with another soldier who took him inside. He opened a heavy gate that separated the palace from a large yard and they entered what looked to be a guest house, but it was long, with many doors. The windows were covered by curtains on the inside and from the outside you could tell this was only a long row of rooms where the palace guards lived. The soldier took him to one of the rooms in the middle of the building and knocked. A voice answered, inviting them in and he opened the door, showing the old man inside. He turned around and tipping his helmet went back to his post.

Hesitating, Gumpen entered the room and stopped in the doorway. He looked inside and as the voice called again, he stepped in. The room was small, but comfortable and tidy. It had a small closet at the far end and from it a young man came out wiping his hands. He stopped surprised and somewhat uneasy when he saw the old man. The two men looked at each other not saying anything. After the awkward moment of silence, the younger man stepped forward and closed the door. He turned around to look at his guest and in a low voice he greeted him.

"Good day, Father. May the Ancestors keep you safe!" The old man did not answer, but instead rushed toward him and tried to shake his hand. The other man took a step back and snapped.

"What are you doing here, Father? Why did you come?" The old man stopped and looked at him in shock.

"I came to take you home, Finup. Your mother is not well and she wants you to come back home. You brother and sister miss you, too." He stopped again and looked at his eldest son who was now looking down.

"You are coming home with me, aren't you?" Hope was in his voice and he tried to look his son in the eye, only he kept looking down. He waited for an answer, but as it did not come, he moved closer to him.

Suddenly, the young man looked up at him and started talking.

"You must be tired, Father. Have a seat and I will bring you some food and something to drink." He turned on his heels and went into the closet. The clatter of plates and glasses stopped suddenly and the young man came back empty handed and looked at his father again.

"Why did you come here, Father," he started again, bitterly. "I told you in the letter that my life is now here, in the Big City. I will not come back to Nill. I *cannot* come back. My friends are here and my future is here, too. I am respected and people look up to me. Back . . . *there*, the only thing I knew was working the land and loading carts in the fall. Here I learned new things. In Nill, I was not allowed to go anywhere, here, I am free to go anywhere I please and meet anybody I like. This is the life I want, this is the future I had been dreaming about." He stopped and looked back at his father. "I am *not* coming back with you. You took the trip in vain and there is nothing you could tell me that would make me change my mind."

CHAPTER 17

The Pariah

Ronden was sitting at the table looking at the fire crackling in the fireplace, lost in thought. He heard a knock at the door and stood up slowly. He opened it and his old friend, Khiran was standing there alone, looking cold. He opened the door wider and gestured him to come in. He entered quietly and found a seat by the fireplace. Khiran was the first to talk.

"Ronden, *he* is getting closer to the borders. We cannot keep the secret anymore. I know we took a vow a long time ago not to talk about this as long as we live, but now everything is changed. Our land is in danger, our families are in danger. We need to do something."

As the other man did not say anything, he continued.

"We need to go to the palace and tell the King about what we have done. He will understand and he will forgive us." Silence filled the room and he looked at his friend who said nothing, but kept staring at the fire. Suddenly, he stood up and put some more wood in the fireplace, poking the charred pieces to get the fire going. Flames surrounded the dry logs and the light shone on the man's face. His eyes were filled with sadness and he turned to his friend who was patiently waiting for him to decide.

"I will go the palace tomorrow and tell the King all about it. We have to help him defeat Finup and we are the only ones who know how." Khiran stood up and got closer to Ronden.

"I will come with you, old friend, we both will tell the King about our secret and how to use the Royal Dagger to stop this madness."

"I will go alone, Khiran, it is my fault that he has turned the evil man he is now. I allowed him to leave Bridd, although I promised the King to keep everybody safe and bring you all home."

Khiran shook his head, interrupting him. "I am coming to. We are both responsible for this. I will not let you take the blame alone."

Brodin was getting close to the city and as the first houses started to appear in the distance he spurred the horse. He had to get the message and the necklace to the King as soon as possible, his Master told him. Their lives depended on it. The horse was covered in foam and the man could feel it struggling to keep up the pace. He pulled the reins and the horse stopped. They were close to the palace now and he realised that the horse will not be able to carry him—it was exhausted. He dismounted and pulled the animal behind him to a house and called to the man in the yard.

"My Lord, I need your help, I am bringing a message to your King and my horse is too tired to take me there. Please give me yours."

The man came closer to the gate and looked suspiciously at the soldier: he looked tired and was covered in dust and sweat. His horse was barely standing and froth was coming out of his mouth.

"What kind of message are you bringing him and who is it from?" the man asked over the gate, not opening it.

"I come from across the border and I was a soldier in the Emperor's army. My Captain, Marden sent me here with a message for the King and I need to meet with him as soon as possible. Our lives depend on in." He let go of the reins and sat down on the bench by the fence. Hearing the name Marden made the man even more curious and he opened the gate to have a better look at the soldier.

"Did you say *Marden*? You say that *he* sent you? Where is he? Is he still alive?" Then he turned suddenly and called to someone in the house.

"Father, come outside, there is someone here who knows Master Marden." The door opened and an old man came out looking amused and surprised at the same time.

"What are you talking about? Marden is long gone, he died years ago. Who is that saying that he has a message from him?" The soldier stood up and bowed his head.

"I know Master Marden—he was my Capitan in the Emperor's army and sent me to meet your King to give him a message. Here is the letter!" He took the bundle from inside of his coat and showed it to them.

"Please, I have to get to the palace, there is no time to waste," he shouted and grabbing the reins of the horse tried to mount it. But the horse wouldn't move, its legs were shaking and it whinnied weakly.

Desperate, the soldier left the horse and started toward the palace, but he was as exhausted as the animal and after a few steps fell to the ground. The two men ran after him and lifted him up.

"There, there young man, we will help you, no need to get yourself killed." The older man turned to his son.

"Bridon, go saddle the horses. We are going to the palace. Let Khiran know and ask him to come and join us. The kingdom needs us and it is time we did our duty."

Night has fallen and Mortor was not back yet. None of his men were back and Marden started to worry. Rotin showed and he too, was worried. He didn't hear back from any of the men who went back to get their dead and injured back to the city. Nobody knew anything about Johanna either, she went alone to the enemy camp to find Finup and take the Ring back.

"How long has it been since they left, Marden? I think we should go after them and see what is keeping them."

Marden shook his head.

"Johanna said we should get everybody ready to leave if she does not return by morning. We will wait until then to see if she makes it back. But I am more worried about Mortor. He should have been back by now. His men returned with the first wagons.

The others should have followed shortly after, but nobody is back yet."

He turned to his friend and looked sadly at him.

"Why do you thing Finup has changed so much lately, Rotin. He was not a bad man when we left Nill all those years ago. What turned him into a traitor?" He stopped and shook his head. Rotin sat down next to him and patted him on the back.

"Marden, there is nothing we can do about him. We need to keep the people safe and that may mean to flee Mortoria and maybe never come back. It seems we were meant to be running all our lives, never to be able to settle anywhere. Now that we have to leave these places too, who knows where we will end up?"

Marden stood up and got his sword.

"I will get a few men and go see what happened to Mortor. Just like Johanna said, if we do not return by morning, get everybody out of here. Look after my family for me, Rotin and may the Ancestors keep you safe, my friend."

The battle field looked deserted and eerily quiet. Marden looked around to see if Mortor or any of his men were still around and the torches shone light only on dead bodies lying on the ground. No sign of his master and he had this bad feeling something has happened to him. He quietly gestured to his companions to get back when he heard a faint moan coming from behind. He turned and asked one of the soldiers to bring the torch closer. The light shone on a body half buried under some branches and leaves and they all rushed to help him out.

The man was badly wounded and they were surprised he had lasted that long: his face was bloodless, even in that dim light it looked as white as paper and his purple lips could hardly move.

"They have him, they have ambushed us and took Mortor," he said faintly. "Finup's people have taken him to the General's camp and killed us all."

Marden kneeled down next to the man who was hardly breathing. "We will take you back to the city, my friend, and you will be all right. Save your strength. You will tell us all about it when we arrive home."

The man grabbed Marden's hand and with a lot of effort he whispered.

"You are too kind Master Marden, but I will go to meet the Ancestors soon. They have been waiting for some time now and they only allowed me to live so that I can tell you about Master Mortor. Go and rescue him Master, they are evil people and they have to be stopped." With that he let out a long breath and his hand let go of Marden's. The others kneeled down beside him and said a prayer.

Marden stood up angrily and kicked the ground. So many innocent people have died because of *him* and he felt so helpless!

"Why do you allow for this to happen? How can I stop him? Tell me what to do!" His angry cry stirred some birds that flew scared in the night. His men looked at him sadly and started quietly to remove the mud and leaves from the body of their fellow. Gently, they lifted him and placed him on the back of one of the horses. Grabbing the reins, they started back home. Marden straightened his tunic and followed them. He mounted his horse and spurred him into a gallop, leaving the others behind. He was too angry and powerless about all of this and he needed to be alone.

The sun was rising and Mortor was hurting. But it was not physical pain that he was feeling. It was the thought of him not being able to get back to his people and warn them about the attack. He could not protect his people from the traitor Finup and that hurt him deeply. He had played them and now he was his hostage. He suddenly remembered about Johanna and how she resisted the torture. He tried to sit up to look for her but he could only see a few men lying lifeless in the corner of the tent. She was not there with him and his heart sank. What if she died during the torture? Or maybe they killed her because she did not want to give up the secret of the Ring?

Finup tried to use it on him last night to make him tell the secrets of Mortoria and its protector, but it didn't work. Finup had become enraged because he could not subdue him and make him do what he wanted. Mortor knew why and wished he could tell him that he was powerless as long as his intentions were to use it for his evil purpose. Mortor's heart, on the other hand, was pure and he sincerely cared about his people, so the Ring would not hurt him. Unfortunately in his enemy's hands the Ring was still powerful. He could control the evil ones with it, like the General.

Mortor tried to stand up, but his legs were tied up too tight. He was about to give up, when he saw the flap move slowly. He looked around for something to help him defend himself, but then he realised his hands were tied at the back—the tightness of the bound had made them numb and he could hardly feel them. To his surprise a gloved hand he recognised held the door open and two men entered the tent. Marden and Rotin smiled and rushed to him. They grabbed the man gently and stood him up. Cutting the ropes binding his legs made him stagger and losing his balance, he fell to the ground. Marden lifted him back on his feet and cut the ropes tying his hands.

Rubbing his wrists to get the blood flowing again, he looked at the two and smiled sadly.

"Did you find Johanna? He caught her last night and tried to make her give up the secret of the Ring. Do you know where she is?" Rotin looked down and answered in a soft voice.

"We found her, but she is badly hurt, My Lord. He tortured her and she resisted . . . but I don't think she will make it." He paused and looked at Marden.

"It is our fault he got the Ring, Master Mortor. He somehow found out about its powers and he tricked us into believing he is the right person to protect the city. We *helped* him become the Ring Bearer. We did not know what he was up to until it was too late. I am so sorry, My Lord." Sadness and desperation filled his voice and Mortor looked at him.

"You couldn't have known what he was up to, Marden. He tricked me too *and* the Council members into giving him the Ring, so you are not responsible for any of this. He is an evil man and somebody needs to stop him." He straightened his coat and turned toward the exit.

"We need to stop him. Even if I will lose my life doing it, I will not allow him to take over Mortoria and my people. You two go back to the city and get everybody ready for battle." None of the two men moved so he looked at them inquisitively.

"What are you waiting for? You need to hurry. Time is running out."

Marden stepped forward and looked straight at him with fierce determination in his eyes.

"Mortor, we are not going anywhere. If you stay, we stay! We are *your people* now, and it is our responsibility to look after the city just like it is yours. We can help and you have to let us do it." Rotin joined him and the two men looked so determined that Mortor felt his strength coming back.

"All right, then," he said, "let's go get rid of evil and get back what is rightfully ours."

CHAPTER 18

The Battle of Mortoria

Finup was lying on the bed, covered in fur blankets thinking about Mortor and Johanna. They had welcomed him all those years ago and now he had turned against them and their people. The feelings he had were not of remorse, but somehow of empowerment: he had been able to ignore the fact that they have been his friends. When he was torturing Johanna into telling him more about the powers of the Ring he felt elation, not pity. When Mortor asked him to let her go and take him instead, he had this powerful urge to hurt her more.

It felt strange that he was not worried about these feelings; others may have thought it was wrong to have such feelings and would try to understand why he was enjoying hurting people, but for some reason he was content, even happy with that. The door to the tent opened and Gampill entered bowing humbly.

"My Lord, what do you want me to do with the bodies of the two traitors? Should I send them back to their people or should we leave them to the crows to feast on?" Finup did not answer and he turned to leave when he heard the crooning voice asking him to come back.

"We will take their bodies back to the city. I want everybody to see what happens to people who do not bow to me." He stopped enjoying his words and as the General turned again to leave, he called him back.

"Bring the other two to my tent. And get everybody ready. When the sun is up, we are going back to the city. The people of Mortoria need to know who their new Master is." Gampill left the tent and Finup looked after him arrogantly. *He* was the new Master and he had to show his new powers.

Marden had returned and Rotin was waiting for him in the council chambers. He had heard about Mortor and he too felt angry and powerless. After all, Finup had been their friend and they all left their homes together all those years ago. They have shared everything: good or bad and they thought they knew each other. But it turned out they did not know anything about him. What made him so angry? Why did he change so? He had no answers to these questions and neither did Marden. He heard the door slam and stood up. Marden and a couple of people entered the room and sat down quietly. They had to decide what to do—they could not leave Mortor in Finup's hands. On top of that, they hadn't heard anything from Johanna and they feared she had a similar fate—she went all alone in the enemy's camp.

Rotin grabbed his sword and looked at the others.

"We have to go find Mortor and bring him back. We have to at least try." Marden did not say anything but he could tell he agreed with him. The look in his eyes told him he was ready to sacrifice his life to save Mortor and Johanna's.

"Bring our horses, Parnat, and let the other council members know we are leaving. Marden and I will bring them back no matter how dangerous it is." Marden stood up, grabbed his gear and headed for the door. He turned toward the other people—his companions and friends—and lowering his eyes whispered.

"We brought him here and we are the ones who endangered your lives; we have to stop Finup from hurting anybody else. If we do not return by the time the sun sets, leave Mortoria and find a safe place for our families. You deserve to have a good and safe life. Farewell!"

The camp was close now and the two men stopped the horses to a trot. Rotin stopped his horse and dismounted, grabbing the reins of the horse. Marden looked at him inquisitively.

"Why are we stopping here, Rotin? We need to go inside the camp and find Mortor and Johanna. He probably has them and I pray they are still alive. Last time I saw him, he was determined to take over Gampill's army and come back to take over Mortoria. He has the Ring and we don't know how its power helps him. Maybe he has used it already."

Rotin looked up at him and then at the camp. He shook his head and pulled the reins. The horse snorted softly and followed him. Marden dismounted quickly and ran after his friend. He caught up with him and grabbed him by the arm.

"Rotin, what is going on? Do you know something I don't? Why are we *walking* to the camp?"

As he did not answer, Marden grabbed the reins and pulled the horse to a stop.

"Talk to me, my friend. What is it?" Not looking up, Rotin started sadly.

"The Ring gives him the power to subdue anybody and by now he most likely got Gampill under his control. If Mortor did not bow, he probably killed him. I am almost certain Mortor didn't give up the secret of the Ring. He would sacrifice anybody for that, he has sworn it. And Johanna knows it too." He stopped and looked at his friend.

"He is very dangerous now, Marden. If I go to the camp, I will tell him that I have left Mortoria and came to join him and his army. I will have to fight in his army and become just like him, if I want to save everybody. I will have to become evil, just like him if I what to stop him. I will have to pay for what I have done and I am ready to be a villain if I can stop him. And I have to somehow persuade him to go back to Bridd."

At the mention of the name, Marden jumped and looked at him frightened.

"How do you know about Bridd? Who told you about it?" His face was pale and his body cringed. He moved closer to Rotin and grabbed him by the shoulders, shaking him.

"How do you know about Bridd, Rotin? Did you have the dreams, too? Did you start to remember who we are, too?"

Rotin looked up at him, smiling sadly. "So, you know about Bridd, don't you, Marden. When did you start having the dreams? When he left the city and turned against the Council? Or was it after he had stolen the Ring?"

Marden smiled back and stopped. "I started having the dreams after he stole the Ring, but I did not know what to make of them, until he attacked the city. It was then, that I had this vision about the Big City and I saw the faces of my parents. I realised who I was and what I had to do." He stopped to catch his breath and continued.

"You are right, *we*—you are not alone in this Rotin, we will go together—we have to go to him and somehow persuade him to go to Bridd. We have to bring him close to the Dagger, maybe its powers will cancel the Ring's and make him powerless."

Determined, the men mounted their horses and spurred them. They had to hurry, the sooner they got to the camp, the better chance to save Mortor and Johanna they had.

Two armoured soldiers pushed Marden and Rotin inside the tent. They smiled and bowed with respect and that made Finup stand up.

"What are you two doing here? I can have you killed for trying to help Mortor and Johanna escape and if my soldiers wouldn't have caught you, you would have managed that."

Marden stepped forward and looked him in the eyes.

"My Lord, we did not want to help them escape, we just wanted to *trick* them into believing we are helping them escape. We wanted to gain their trust to make them tell us more about the Ring. We were very close to finding that out, but your soldiers found us and brought us to you." Finup raised his hand and Marden stopped. He moved closer and looked at him with curiosity mixed with admiration.

"Is that why you came here, to find out more about the power of the Ring?" He stopped for a moment, like thinking about it and looking at Marden, asked. "And did you?" Rotin moved closer to them and added.

"We only found out that the power of the Ring is complimented by a dagger. Mortor said that the two together give the owner enough power to win all battles and become the master of the world." He stopped and looked at Finup.

"The dagger," he repeated pacing about, "I don't remember him talking about any dagger, are you sure it was a dagger and not a sword?"

Then he turned around with a sudden move and looked suspiciously at the two men.

"You are lying, aren't you? You are trying to make me think that the power of the Ring alone is not enough for me to control everybody. You are liars, you are trying to trick me into giving up taking over Mortoria and go somewhere else. Is that it? Tell me, you traitor!" His voice was now hoarse and his eyes yellow with fury. But Rotin held his look and smiled defiantly.

"Why would I lie, Finup, what would I gain from telling you about the dagger and the combined powers of the two? You could have had us killed by now, but you did not. Why is that? Because you believe us? You *did* know about the dagger, didn't you?" Finup stopped in front of him and growled.

"My name is *Emperor* Finup, and yes, I did know about the dagger, but I couldn't find out where it was. If you want to keep your lives, you'd better know where it is. Tell me, where is it?" He stopped again and turning quickly around, got his sword. He grabbed Marden by his coat and holding him, pushed its tip on his neck.

"Where is the dagger, Marden? Did Mortor tell you before he died?" Marden smiled at him, just like his friend Rotin and snarled.

"Yes, I do, but I will not tell you unless you release their bodies and leave Mortoria be."

Finup looked at them surprised once more and let out a cackle.

"What is it with you two? Why do you care about Mortoria? Is there anybody there that you care about? Eh, Rotin, is there someone you want to save from my wrath?" He turned to Marden.

"What about you, do you have a *loved one* you want to keep safe?" Laughing, he turned around and put the sword back.

"All right, I will leave Mortoria be. Now you tell me where the dagger is."

"The dagger is in the Kingdom of Bridd, on the other side of the mountains, past the lands of Kunada and Robania. It is kept in the dungeons of the palace. You will have to take over the city to find it, but it shouldn't be a problem. They do not have an army and they have never fought in battle. They are peaceful people and they will probably surrender without a fight."

Marden stopped and looked at Finup again. He had given him the details and now he hoped that this will convince him to leave the city be, but he knew him all too well: in the morning he will order the attack. His hope was that everybody would be gone by then and Finup will not find anyone there to slaughter.

It was finally morning and Finup was ready. His horse was saddled and his sword and body armour polished. He put it on with the help of his man-servant and grabbed the sword and his helmet and stepped out of the tent. The General was waiting outside and when he saw him he moved closer and bowed. He pointed at two horses behind the tent that had two bundles on their backs. The bodies of Mortor and Johanna, wrapped in white cloths had been laid on the saddles. Finup smiled defiantly and walked slowly, enjoying the view.

"I am taking you two home, my *friends*," he mocked, pretending to caress the bodies, "you will be together with your families and friends. I kept my promise." He turned to the general and shouted. "Let's get ready, it's time to go. Bring Marden and Rotin over. I need to talk to them before we leave." He turned on his heels and asked for his horse. A soldier brought it and he mounted it with a quick jump. As he was pulling the reins to turn the horse around, he saw the two men approaching.

"You two will lead the battle to take over Mortoria. You, Marden will be the captain of the first battalion and you, Rotin will be his second. Take them!" The two lowered their heads and followed the soldiers. The first part of their plan succeeded—they were joining him in his campaign; now they only had to work on the second part—to convince him to go to Bridd. They knew Finup lied when he promised to not attack Mortoria, they only hoped the people had left and they would not find anybody there.

Marden was thinking about how furious Finup will be when he will find the city deserted. He will probably hurt them, but it was all worth it if they wanted to save their friends and families. He promised himself that no matter what it would take, he will bring justice to Mortor and Johanna and to the people of Mortoria who had taken them in and trusted them with their lives.

They mounted their horses and took lead of their men. The ride is short and since the horses were rested, they will cover the distance in about half an hour. The loud trot of the hooves filled the air and the orders shouted around the camp echoed. Marden said a quick prayer and spurred the horse. He called to his men and looked to the right at his friend Rotin. With a nod they moved ahead and the army followed. May the Ancestors help them and bring peace to their troubled souls! Nothing in the world will make them forgive themselves, but they had to play this dangerous game if they wanted to stop Finup.

They were there! The city looked deserted and Marden let out a sigh of relief—they managed to leave. Rotin joined him shortly and looked around with a triumphant smile on his face. Gampill caught up with them and barked.

"Where is everybody? Did you tell them we were coming?" He dismounted and started looking around, opening doors and kicking open gates.

"They are all gone, the city is deserted! You, go tell the Emperor that these two betrayed us. Get them and tie them up," he shouted at another pair of soldiers. The two rushed to get them, but Marden took his sword out and prepared to defend himself. Rotin joined him and back to back the two turned around menacingly.

"You have no power to order us around, Gampill, you are no better than us. It is Finup who will decide if we are traitors or not. Go and get him, Sarden. Tell him what happened and that we need to talk to him." As he hesitated, Rotin shouted.

"Go, you will be all right!" The soldier looked at the General and then back at Rotin. He started running and soon after Finup was following him. The soldier looked terrified, but seemed to be unhurt. Finup dismounted and another soldier rushed to get his horse. He looked at the two men with their swords drawn and at Gampill.

"What is going on here," he asked in his crooning voice. "Why did you sent for me?" He turned to Marden and asked again. "What do you want? Who are you two fighting?" Marden let his sword down and approached him.

"Gampill thinks we are traitors. He thinks that we have told the people of Mortoria to leave. What do you think, My Lord? Did we betray you?" His voice was getting louder as he talked and everybody was listening quietly. Gampill looked at Finup for approval, but his master did not say anything. Instead he took off his helmet and moved closer to the General.

"I knew the city would be deserted, I have lived here for many years, Gampill. I know these people—I did not expect to find anybody here. They are proud but smart people and they know when to give up. Take the bodies of the two and put them in the city hall. Then get everybody ready to move out. We are heading for the Kingdom of Bridd. They have something there that I need and we have to go get it." With that he turned to Rotin and snarled.

"You'd better be right about this, or else I will have your head for my trophy." Rotin looked at him and then at Marden.

"I am right, and you know it my Lord. We wouldn't be here if you didn't trust us. We are ready to take your army to Bridd. We know the way, better than anybody else." He stopped and turned to Marden who was listening quietly.

"The two of us will lead the way, if you would let us, My Lord," he added and Marden nodded in his support.

"We need to hurry, My Lord," Marden added and grabbed the reins of his horse.

With a defiant look, he turned towards Gampill and spat the words out.

"You can join us too, Gampill, if you want," he mocked. "Our Master trusts us more than you do, as we do believe in the power of the Ring. We know *It* will keep us safe in our travels. You should do to. You will soon see Its powers at work." He brought Finup's horse around and helped him get on.

"Let's go, Master. We have no time to lose." The three men mounted and shouted to the others to follow.

The second part of their plan has worked. Now, they only had to play into Finup's game. Soon, they will be reunited with their brothers and hoped that with their help, Finup's tyranny will be stopped. They hoped the Ancestors will help them and guide them through this.

CHAPTER 19

Revelations

"You have to take the necklace and keep it safe; keep it away from *him*," the young woman whispered. "He cannot have it. If he finds out about *it* he will want to get it and that would allow him to control everybody." Marden took the necklace and hid it inside of his tunic. He took Johanna's hand in his and gave it a gentle squeeze.

"I will protect it with my own life. Now let's take you back home so you can rest." The man lifted her carefully and put her on the cot. Rotin covered her with a blanket and turned toward Mortor.

"She isn't going to make it, is she?" he whispered. He looked at her and then back at his friends.

"He killed her, didn't he? He tortured her to make her give up the secret of the Ring, but she didn't say anything. Mortor, we need to take her away from here. She needs to be properly buried so she can join the Ancestors. We owe that to her." His voice broke and he hid his face away from her.

"There is nothing we can do, Rotin," Mortor said. "She sacrificed her life to save us and our people. You have to accept that. It was her choice. But yes, you are right, we have to give her a proper burial. First we need to try and get the Ring back. You stay here and look after her—someone has to be with her when time comes. Marden and I will go look for Finup. He has the Ring and if he didn't use it on Gampill already, he will do it soon. He needs him under his control so he can take over his army." He turned to Johanna who was lying on the cot with her eyes closed.

"We have to go, my daughter, we have to try to get the Ring back. You stay here and rest. Rotin will stay with you. We will be back as soon as we can." He turned to leave when he heard the woman's weak voice calling for him.

"Master Mortor, he *has* used it, I was there when he did and I witnessed Its powers. Now Gampill is under his influence. There is nothing you can do. He will not give it up and you cannot take it away from him. He is too powerful. You need to keep the necklace hidden. He cannot have both of them. I will soon go to the Ancestors and I will look after you. Please get away from here and keep everybody safe." She stopped exhausted and closed her eyes again.

Rotin looked at the others and got closer to her, crouching down next to her bed.

"Milady, there is something you need to know. There is a dagger that may cancel the Ring's power. This can only happen when the person who got it either stole it or obtain it by force. The dagger is in a place called Bridd. This was written in the sacred scrolls kept in the hidden vault of the Council Hall of Mortoria. If we cannot get the Ring back, we have to somehow persuade Finup to go to Bridd." He laughed sadly.

"He will be easy to persuade, his hunger for power is too big for him now. We will keep the necklace safe and will take you home like we promised. You need to rest now, let us worry about it."

Gumpen looked at the necklace once more and with shaking hands he lifted it and showed it to Rubana. The woman started crying quietly and stood up. Randan stood up in respect but she gestured him to sit back down. The old woman opened a wooden cupboard in the corner of the room, took out a metal box and gave it to her husband. He opened it and rummaged through it looking for something. He seemed to have found it and stopped, looking up.

"This is the letter that my grandmother gave me when she joined the Ancestors. She told me that the necklace is an heirloom from her grandmother, a woman named Ronda Norria. The village Ronda was named after her. People say she was the daughter of King Nill and before he went to the Ancestors he gave each of his children a magic heirloom. I have given it to my first born, Finup when he turned of age, but he is gone now and when he left Nill, he took it with him. How did you come to have it, My Lord?" he asked with shaking voice.

Young Gleal looked at the two old people and shrugged smiling.

"I don't know where it came from, Master Gumpen, my father gave it to me together with this letter to bring it over to you and ask you to come to the Big City. We need you there to help stop the Emperor from invading our lands." He stopped, embarrassed a little for not being able to give him more information. He wondered if his Father actually knew where the necklace came from.

He continued, looking at the old man.

"Master Gumpen, read the letter, maybe the answer is written in there." He waited for the man to open it but to his surprise, he gave it back to him, smiling.

"My Lord, I am old and I can hardly see anymore. You can read it for me." He stood up and handed the letter to Gleal who took it, broke the seal and started reading.

Master Gumpen, I hope my letter finds you in good health. I am writing to you during hard times. I have found out in the Book of Wisdom that the Emperor who is threatening our lands and has killed and pillaged countless villages and cities is someone born in Nill, fifty years ago. You have lived in Nill all your life and I need you to come to the capital city to help me find out who he is. I am also sending this necklace with my son—it is said one just like it belonged to him. I beg you to join my son and return to the city. You are the only one who can help us. King Lade-Gleal.

As soon as Gleal finished, the old man took a deep breath and stood up, leaning on his cane.

"I know who this man is, My Lord. He is my long lost son, Finup. And I know how he can be stopped. I only wish we had enough time to get to the capital." He turned toward his wife and spoke softly.

"I have to go Ruba, I have to stop him and try one more time to bring him home. Our King needs me now. Pack a few things for me. I will be gone for a while." The woman stood up and grabbed a small pack hanging on a nail behind the front door and left the men. They could hear her opening and closing drawers and doors and soon she reappeared carrying the pack. It seemed to be heavy and Randan jumped up to take it from her, but she gently pushed his hand away and gave it to Gumpen.

"There is no need to protect me, son. Our people need our help and we will go together to the city." She turned toward her husband who smiled at her encouragingly.

"We are *both* going to try and stop Finup, My Lord. We are his parents and we know him best. Randan, go bring the wagon and harness the horse. We need to leave as soon as possible. We have a long way to go."

The King was tired but he had to finish the chapter about the true heirs. It was the key of how to defeat the Emperor.

Each of the three brothers inherited the magic gifts from their father, but they were in fact four talismans, known as the 'Foursome': the Twin Necklaces were to be given to twins or their magic power would be ripped in two; the stone was the Wisdom Stone and it gave great wisdom to its owner; the Royal Dagger's hilt was covered by precious stones and their joined power gave its owner big strength; the last one, a ring, was the Sacred Ring and it had the power to change people's lives. They had been passed along from generation to generation and each of the talismans was tied to a scroll telling its owner how to use it. How King Nill came in the possession of the Stone, nobody remembered. It belonged to the third son, Kostan, but somehow it ended up with his brother Bird's descendants.

Soon after their father's passing, the two younger sons left the Kingdom of Bridd and wandered around the world. But just like the prophecy said, as soon as they stepped outside of their homeland, they forgot who they were and where their families lived. After many years, Dorden decided to settle in the land of Kunada and Larden, in Larmar. There, they both became influent people and everybody respected them for their honesty and kindness.

Many generations have passed and just like King Nill's only daughter, Ronda, her descendants gave up the busy court life and settled in the village of Nill. She has passed on the necklace she had inherited to her descendants and the last to have it was her great-grandson, Gumpen, but nobody knows what happened to the Royal Dagger. It is said that an evil uncle had stolen it from the palace and it lost its magical powers. The stone was passed on from heir to heir in the land of Larmar and it had helped people there live good and prosperous lives. The second necklace, inherited by the twin brother, Dorden is now in the possession of his great-grand daughter Johanna, daughter of Torban. She lives in her great-grandfather's homeland of Kunada.

The King stopped and turned the page. There it was—the timeline showing the genealogy of his forefathers, from the very beginning to his father's time. His name was not there yet, and he assumed it will be added when he will join the Ancestors. The paper listed the names of his forefathers and his dead relatives, but why was Gumpen's name there? He knew he was still alive. He knew nothing about the others; his father did not mention them in his lifetime as he did not say anything about the *Foursome*.

His heart jumped suddenly—but what if Gumpen had died? What if the others died too and now the gifts were lost? How is he going to fight the Emperor? But then why did the Spirit tell him to send for Gumpen if he was already with the Ancestors? Something did not make sense and he called the Spirit.

"The timeline in the book does not make sense, Spirit. Why is my name not here? Why are Gumpen's and Johanna's names in here, but not mine? Am I not one of the heirs? I come from the line of King Nill, the adopted son of King Rondal and Queen Minada. My grandfather is Nill Sunden and he is one of the four children of King Nill." He waited, but the Spirit did not answer. He turned to the book and looked at the timeline again and saw the name Ropettian, as the great-grandson of Nill Larden, King Nill's youngest son. Brohan was meeting him at the borders—he remembered the name the Spirit had told him, last time he was reading the Book. Something was not right about this timeline and he did not have time to wait for the Spirit to clarify it for him. He had to get ready for the meeting, Brohan must be on his way back already and his son Gleal had sent word about his imminent return. He stood up and headed for the door, while the Book closed behind him. Just as he was taking the torch off the floor, the Spirit called him.

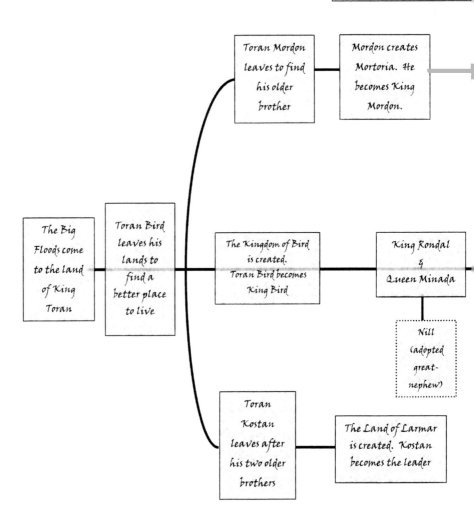

Toran Mordon leaves to find his older brother

Mordon creates Mortoria. He becomes King Mordon.

The Big Floods come to the land of King Toran

Toran Bird leaves his lands to find a better place to live

The Kingdom of Bird is created. Toran Bird becomes King Bird

King Rondal & Queen Minada

Nill (adopted great-nephew)

Toran Kostan leaves after his two older brothers

The Land of Larmar is created. Kostan becomes the leader

Toran Bird inherited the Royal Dagger and the Twin Necklaces
Toran Mordon inherits the Sacred Ring
Toran Kostan inherits the Stone of Wisdom

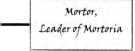

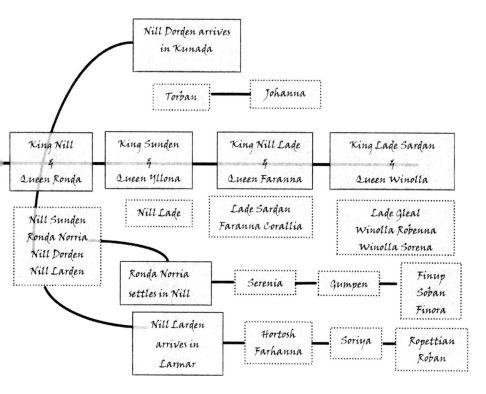

Mortor,
Leader of Mortoria

Nill Dorden arrives
in Kunada

Torban — Johanna

King Nill & Queen Ronda	King Sunden & Queen Yllona	King Nill Lade & Queen Faranna	King Lade Sardan & Queen Winolla

Nill Sunden
Ronda Norria
Nill Dorden
Nill Larden

Nill Lade

Lade Sardan
Faranna Corallia

Lade Gleal
Winolla Robenna
Winolla Sorena

Ronda Norria
settles in Nill — Serenia — Gumpen — Finup / Soban / Finora

Nill Larden
arrives in
Larmar — Hortosh / Farhanna — Soriya — Ropettian / Roban

"You will understand how the timeline works soon, King Lade. Now go and meet your people. It is time to get ready. The Emperor is preparing for battle and you need to gather everybody to face him. I will be watching over you."

The King turned and opened the door. Yes, he had to get ready, his people needed to find out what was going on and he had to send messengers to the farthest corners of the kingdom to let everybody know of the dangers. And he did not have too much time.

Ropettian and his brother stood by the table and looked at the small wooden box, with the bird engraved on it. Could the box have the key to the vault in the city hall? Could the old inhabitants of the city have hidden it in the garden to keep it safe from their enemies? One of the Ropé's companions whispered.

"You should open it, maybe the key is inside." The others murmured in agreement. Ropé turned to his brother and handed him a knife. "You open it, brother. You are the city's Head Councillor." Roban took the knife from his brother and tried to pry the box open. But the box seemed to be jammed. Then Ropé took the knife and tried, but he was not able to open it either. Everybody looked at the two men curiously and offered to help, but as they tried, none managed to even scratch the box.

Disappointed, some of them started to leave and as the door opened, Ropé's daughters came in giggling. Trimana, the first to be born, saw the box and grabbed it. She shook it and a magical sound came out of it. The other daughter, Solanna, grabbed the box and tugged. The two girls started fighting over it, but they lost their grip and it dropped on the floor.

Ropé hurried to them, but before he could get it, the box tumbled around and hit the leg of the table. The lid sprang open. Out of it fell a key and a bunch of scrolls tied together with a ribbon. The girls let out a delighted cry at the sight of the things and tried to grab them, but Ropé was quicker. Right then, Tracia came running inside and saw them wrestling with their father who was laughing and was trying to hold the things over his head out of their reach. She grabbed them and tried to take them out of the house, but they wiggled wildly in her arms and she put them down. The men who stayed behind laughed at the sight and tried to grab the girls and settle them down. Tracia had finally managed to grab them by their arms and was headed to the door when Ropé called her.

"Let them stay, without them we would not have been able to open the box. They must have done something to it when they played with it, so they might as well stay. We will have to see what these scrolls are and then try the key in the vault." He then turned to the girls.

"You girls helped us open the box so you can stay and listen, but no touching, all right?" The girls giggled and sat down with their mother. The others craned their necks to see the scrolls and Ropé united the ribbon. The four yellow parchments bore the image of a bird on the wax seal and Ropé opened one. Something like a poem was on the first one and he started reading.

> *They are twins, born from burning light.*
> *As they spread their wings ready to take off,*
> *Their heads stand up high.*

The poem did not make any sense, so he opened the next scroll. Another poem was written and he read it.

> *The blade is not sharp and*
> *You'll not use it to hurt your enemy,*
> *But to show your rightful place in your family.*

It still did not make sense, but this one was talking about something they thought was slightly familiar. He put it on the table next to the other one and opened the third scroll.

> *This circle of life will shine on your hand.*
> *The claw that holds it won't hurt anyone,*
> *But empower you to be just, merciful and kind.*

The poem written on this one seemed to make more sense, but he could not figure out how. He read it again and looked at the people in the room. "Do you understand any of this?"

People shook their heads and he decided to open the last one, when Trimana shouted.

"Riddle! Riddle, daddy!" Ropé turned toward her and his other daughter joined in.

"Riddle! Riddle!"

Traciana looked at them and then she understood.

"Ropé, these are riddles, that's what they're saying. The poems on the scrolls are *riddles*. We have to figure out what they mean. Read the last one!" Ropé grabbed the last scroll and read it quickly.

> *Whoever will have it, will be wise, man or woman.*
> *Its smooth faces shine brightly when danger is close and*
> *Will guide you on the right path if that is what you chose.*

Now *that* made sense, it sounded very familiar and he looked at his wife and brother.

"Do you two think this is what *I* think it is?" Without waiting for their answer he ran to the other room and started looking through a drawer dropping things on the floor as he went through it. With a victorious *Aha!* he grabbed something out of it and returned to the kitchen where everybody was waiting anxiously.

He came back holding a purple gem fastened to a round stand and he showed it to them. He grabbed the paper from the table again and read it while holding the gem. As soon as he finished, sparkles shot out of it and he dropped it. The gem started glowing and a magical music started playing as it continued to sparkle. Then, to everyone's shock it stopped glowing and from its top a ray sprung up. They all backed up and the shape of an old man appeared.

"If you have conjured me, then you must be trying to conjure the magical power of the Stone of Wisdom. You have to know that its power can only be used together with the other talismans. Only together, the *Foursome* will have enough power to help you. You need to find the Dagger, the twin necklaces and the Sacred Ring. If you are in danger, they will give you the strength to overcome it. You have to gather them all and have the rightful owners hold them while you answer the riddles. Only the rightful owners can conjure the magic."

The man stopped and everybody started talking at once asking him questions. But the man continued, ignoring them and they all stopped talking again.

"He who stole the *Foursome* or got them by force, will not be able to use them. They will only be able to control those who are evil and only for as long as they are outside of Bridd. As soon as they crossed the border, their powers will be cancelled and the gifts will become non-magical heirlooms."

As quickly as the man appeared, as quickly he disappeared and the gem stopped glowing. Ropé moved closer carefully and looked at it. The gem was again an ordinary purple jewel sitting on an ordinary stand made of stone. He picked it up gently and put it back on the table. Then he turned to the others.

"We need to see what the key opens and maybe will find out more about the *Foursome* and Bridd." He grabbed the scrolls and headed out, the others following him. Tracia and the girls joined them and the two parents grabbed them and lifted them up in their arms. They were the heroes of the day and as young as they were, they deserved to see everything.

Ronden and Khiran were headed to the palace and their horses were trotting loudly on the stone street. Behind them, Brodin was trying to keep up, but he was exhausted by the long trip and the horse under him felt that and slowed down. From time to time, the other two would stop and wait for him—Brodin was after all the messenger and they had to let him take Marden's message to the King. They stopped for the last time to wait for him—the palace was right ahead. The soldier caught up with them and dismounted. They would walk the last few meters. At the gate, two guards stopped them and asked what they wanted.

"We need to see the King, son," answered Ronden. "This messenger here has important new about the Emperor. He needs to see the King. Tell him that we have a message from the battle field."

The guards looked at each other and one of them called to an older man who seemed to be their superior. He came walking fast and looked at them. He then recognised them and invited them inside. The guards stepped aside and they walked in the palace's front yard leaving the horses outside.

"What brings you here, master Ronden?" asked the man. "And who is this soldier? I do not recognise his uniform." Brodin bowed with respect and answered in his place.

"I have been sent by my Master, Capitan Marden and I bring a message for your King. I have to give it to him as soon as I arrive. My master sends information about the Emperor and how to defeat him."

The Captain of the Guards looked surprised at the mention of the Emperor's name and he looked at the two older men.

"Is it true what he says? Is he really coming from the battle field?" The two nodded and turned to the messenger.

"Show him the letter, Brodin. It has Marden's seal and mark and I know it all too well." The soldier took it out of his tunic and showed it to the guard.

There was the proof: the letter did indeed have Marden's seal—a crowned bird with wings spread. With it, the soldier showed him a small bundle. He did not open it, but the guard didn't need more proof. He asked the three men to wait and called out to one of the guards standing by the palace's door. One of them came running and the older man whispered something in his ear. He then ran back and disappeared inside. After a few minutes he returned and invited them in. Ronden and Khiran nodded at the old guard and gently grabbed Brodin by his arm and led him inside, following the guard.

The King was in the War Room waiting for the messengers. When the guard told him that someone with news from the Emperor's camp was waiting at the gates, he urged him to bring them inside. He understood now that any news about the Emperor will help him prepare for the defence.

A soft knock on the door made him turn his head and called out to them to enter. The guard bowed and invited the three men inside and then turned around to go back to his post. The King stood up to greet them and the men entered.

"Come on in, sit down, you must be tired. I'll have the kitchens bring you some food and something to drink."

Khiran stepped forward and talked first.

"My Lord, we do not have time to rest. The Emperor is getting ready for battle and this young man here has useful information for you. He brings you news from the Emperor's camp and a message from our friend Marden. Marden has left the kingdom a very long time with two others and now they are coming back home." He stopped and turned to the messenger encouraging him to speak.

The young man bowed and took the letter out of his pocket and the bundle and handed them to the King. He took the letter and looked at the seal. He placed it on the table beside him and then opened the bundle. The sight of the necklace made him let out a small cry of surprise and he looked up at the soldier.

"Where did your master get this, soldier? What is your master's name?" The soldier looked surprised at the King and did not answer. Instead, Ronden stepped forward and answered in his place.

"The necklace is an heirloom that a man called *Finup* inherited from his father, My Lord. He must have taken it from him sometime or maybe he has given it to him. We have all travelled together a long time ago and we shared some secrets." The King looked at him and smiled.

"You are mistaken, Master Ronden, this necklace is not the one that Finup inherited. It must come from someone else. Nevertheless, it tells me that this man here is honest and brings me news from the Emperor's camp. I will have a look at the letter, maybe *it* will solve the mystery. Now have him rest and you may go."

Ronden looked at Khiran and as he nodded quietly, he continued.

"We have other news for you, My Lord. We would like to stay a little longer to tell you more about the Emperor's past." As the King looked surprised, Khiran took out another letter he had inside of his coat. The seal of the House of Bridd made the King even more curious but the look on the man's face let him understand that this was not for the messenger's ears, just for him. He called to the guard who was waiting outside and the door opened.

"Take our guest to the kitchens and give him something to eat. Then put him in one of the barracks to rest." He then turned to the tired soldier and smiled.

"Go with him and have something to eat, son, then get some rest. Thank you for your help. My people will be forever grateful for what you have done for us." With a bow, the man turned and followed his guide.

CHAPTER 20

Reunion

Brohan stopped and so did the group of soldiers accompanying him. He turned to the Chief of the Guards and as he came closer, he pointed to a cloud of dust the distance: it was growing and soon they could make out the silhouettes of people riding at the front. They could tell they were coming in fast and dismounted. There were no trees or vegetation and the tired soldiers started to put up some tarps to get some shade for people and horses. One brought some leather bags with water and broke some bread in pieces and handed them over to the men. He offered some water to his master, but he turned him down with a quick hand gesture—the men needed it more than him.

"I hope they are the guests the King wanted us to greet," he told Gardall. You'd better get the men ready, just in case they are vagabonds and we need to defend ourselves. Gardall shouted his orders and the men put down their food and water and grabbed their weapons. Brohan started walking toward the group and stopped a few meters away from the makeshift camp. The dust was sky high now and he could tell that the riders at the front were followed by large wagons pulled by strong horses.

The man leading the party pulled the reins to stop his horse and raised his hand. The drivers pulled the reins and called to the horses. The wagons stopped and the men dismounted. A younger looking man walked forward and joined the leader. From one of the wagons, a woman jumped out and joined the two men. They both walked together and stopped in front on the Councillor.

"I am Ropettian, leader of the people of Larmar and this is my wife, Traciana. That is my brother Roban and these are my daughters." Two young girls showed from behind one of the wagons and approached the group. Brohan turned to his party and told them to put the weapons down and walked toward Ropettian extending his hand and smiling.

"I thought you were some vagabonds roaming these deserted lands. I apologise for the extra precautions. Our trip was long and uneventful, I hope yours was the same. My name is Brohan and I am King Lade-Gleal's First Councillor. This is Gardall, the Chief of the Guards. We have come to meet you and take you home."

Ropé shook his hand and the two men hugged each other like long lost friends. The woman joined them and she too hugged Brohan but the girls only curtsied giggling. The old man shook their hands and bowed to them making them blush.

"We should rest a little and then head back, the King is waiting for you. There is warm food and soft beds for everyone at the palace. As soon we crossed the border into our land we should be safe." He smiled again at the tired people and showed them to the tarp, out of the burning sun.

The wagon was creaking and shaking but the man kept pushing the horse. He was shouting encouragements at it without using the whip and soon they were on the other side of the raging creek. He pulled the reins and the horse stopped, exhausted. Not far away there was a group of houses and Keapock looked at his cousin for approval. He nodded and the young man dismounted and left his horse behind. Soon, he returned with a couple of men and they helped unhitch the tired animal and led it to a stable nearby. Another group of men followed shortly bringing a rested one, hitching it to the wagon.

A couple of women came with some food and water and they helped the old woman climb down from the wagon. She looked tired and cold and they took her inside.

"Master Gumpen, we should get inside too and warm up a little. We can continue our trip after we had something to eat," one of the men called. The old man climbed down slowly and looked at his driver.

"Randan, you and the other men, go and have something to eat, we will join you soon. I need to talk to the young prince." He looked at Gleal and smiled.

"My Lord, we should leave my wife behind and continue our trip. She is too tired to go on."

Right then, the woman came back out and heard him talking.

"I will not be left behind, old man! I may be tired, but I have come all this way and I will not get scared by a few more hours of riding in that shaky wagon of yours." She smiled and turned toward Gleal.

"My Lord, you should go inside and warm up, too. Have something to eat and then we can go on. The men are ready with the horses and as soon as we are finished we can go." Gleal smiled back and entered the house. She sounded just like his mother and he took her advice. He did need a hot drink—the wind and the cold had gotten to him. They were close to home now and his father would not have minded for them to stop for a little while.

As soon as the door closed behind them, the King turned to Ronden and asked him curtly.

"Where did you get this letter? This is my Father's seal. How did it get into your hands?"

Ronden looked back at his master and answered.

"Your father gave it to me, My Lord. He got it from a stranger a long time ago and it tells about the contents of two chests we brought to the palace's dungeons a long time ago. We swore never to talk about it, but times are hard and danger is upon us. I think he wouldn't mind me giving it to you." The King's face lit up and took the letter. He opened it and after reading it, he called to the guard at the door. He entered and the King gestured to him to come in.

"Tramon, I need you to go fetch Rehon and Myrdall. Tell them to meet me in my study." He then turned to the two men and invited them out of the room.

"Come with me. I need your help." The three men left the War Room and headed for the King's private study. It was time to solve one more riddle and he needed all the help he could get.

The King entered the study and called the others inside. Rehon looked at his father as he put an old scroll on the table. Myrdall remained in the corner, not daring to move—this was his first time in the King's private office and he felt overwhelmed by the importance of the moment. Ronden and Khiran stood side by side in the doorway and waited for the King to talk to them. Instead, he gestured to everybody to have a seat on the chairs spread around in the room and closed the door.

Khiran looked around and smiled: he knew this room, he had been here before. Has was only a young man that time, but he remembers it well. His friend Ronden had been there too. The both of them were soldiers in the palace's guards and they had been called in by King Sardan Lade, King Lade's father. King Lade was a young man himself when they met with the old King in his study and he didn't think he would remember them. When he had found out about the mission, Finup asked to be allowed to go with them too and the King had allowed it. A party of five men left the capital city but as they arrived in the village, Finup deserted them and he, Rotin and Marden left their companions to find "adventure". He knows now what kind of *adventure* he found—killing and destroying lives across the lands.

The memories of those times brought back other memories of their good lives as young men, when they started their families and enjoyed having children and grandchildren. But that was about to end now, because they had not been able to keep Finup from leaving Bridd. The secret he and Ronden have been keeping for so long had to be revealed and the King will have to know how they, too, betrayed their people.

"My Lord, we need to tell you about the letter and about why your father asked us to keep our mission a secret. It has to do with the necklace that Marden gave his messenger," Ronden talked for the first time. The King looked curiously at him but invited him to continue.

"A long time ago, when your father was still King of the land, we took a trip to the borders of the kingdom to bring back something that had been stolen from him. At the time, King Sardan, made us swear not to tell anybody about it, but we know now that what we brought back to the palace is connected to the necklace and maybe to a ring that the old kings left to their descendants." The King was now surprised by what the man had said.

"What ring are you talking about? And how did you come to know about it?" It was Khiran's turn to talk and he looked at his friend for approval. He nodded and the man continued.

"Your father called us in and told us that a long time ago, one of his father's distant cousins had stolen a dagger that had been in the family for generations. This cousin had been dead for a long time now, but his son had found the dagger while looking through his father's belongings. He found it in a chest his father had kept in a vault in the basement of his house, together with some scrolls. He now wanted the King to have them and had sent him a message. There were five of us that went on that trip, but only two returned with the two chests. The other three fled the kingdom and never returned. Until now."

Rehon and Myrdall looked at each other and then at the King. What dagger and scrolls were these two men talking about? And how did it relate to the necklace? Or to a ring? Or to the Emperor, for that matter? The King stood up and with him everybody else. He gestured to them to sit back down.

"I think I know what you are talking about, Khiran. I saw the chests in the dungeons recently, sitting in a corner and I remember my Father taking them there. He did not talk about them and when I asked what they were, he did not answer. He told me that it was something related to the Ancestors and I will find out about it in due time." He stopped and grabbed the paper he had placed on his desk and showed it to the two men.

"Is this the letter the cousin's son had sent him?" They nodded.

"I had it in my home, locked up, My Lord," Khiran answered. Then lowered his head and continued. "Finup was on that trip with us and he tried to steal it so he could use the dagger later, but I took it from him when he left Bridd. I also got his necklace and gave it to your father. It belonged to him, not Finup; he was betraying his people and with the two gifts he could have become a very powerful man. We tried to prevent him from becoming that, but we did not succeed." Bitterness was in his voice and his friend pated him sympathetically on the back.

"I am sorry, My Lord, for not being strong enough and for letting him become a murderer." Instead of being angry, the King came from around his desk to look at the two men.

"You have not betrayed anybody, my friends, you did everything you could to protect our lands. The fact that you are here now, helps us find a way of stopping Finup. Now let's get the dagger and the necklaces and see what else we need to save our land."

The guests were here! The King was outside, in front of the palace waiting for them to enter the yard. Brohan came in first and had the guards open the gates. The riders had dismounted and were leading the horses in, with the wagons following. People have started to come to the palace and were waiting respectfully on the sides of the street. The strangers must have been important people if the King was welcoming them like this.

"Welcome, Ropettian, welcome to the City of Bridd, our great-grandparents' house. These are my sons Gleal and Rehon and my eldest daughter Llewella. You must be tired and hungry. Let us show you to your rooms to rest and we can talk later." Ropettian stepped closer to the King and bowed. His wife and brother joined him in the show of respect while his daughters stayed behind waiting for their father's call.

"I thank you for the escort and the warm welcome. We are very honoured to be here. This is my wife Traciana and my brother Roban. Those are my two daughters, Trimana and Solanna. And those are my companions who left our homeland of Larmar to come look for our brothers and sisters. We thank the Ancestors for looking after us on this long journey and for bringing us home." The two men hugged each other and the bystanders cheered—their long lost brothers and sisters were back and it was time for celebration. But the King raised his hand and addressed them.

"Citizens of Bridd, it is time for us to get ready to defend our land. Our brothers and sisters have returned to help us do that. Time for celebration will come, but now we have to all get together and find our swords and armours. It is time to fight for our freedom!"

Silence fell over the crowd and the King looked around at them encouragingly.

"We will be victorious, my friends, we are defending our land, while the enemy is trying to steal what is not his. The Ancestors will look after us and will guide and protect us. Go home and be with your families. We are going to battle soon."

Gumpen was sitting in a chair by the window and was looking down in the street. The guests were coming inside and the crowd was dispersing. Some of the men stayed behind discussing, but he could not hear them. He could only imagine what they were talking about: the preparations for battle. They didn't know who they would be fighting, but he did. It was his son that had turned against his own people and led to all the death and destruction. It was his son who had betrayed his parents and his land.

He turned away from the window and looked at Rubana who was resting on the bed. His stubbornness had cost him his son and her happiness and now here they were, trying to save the kingdom. He hoped they didn't have to go to battle, but the King was convinced there was nothing they could do about it.

They had arrived at the palace the day before and the King welcomed them in his private study. His son, Gleal was accompanying them and they all sat down to talk about the trip. He did not ask anything about the necklace or its powers. Instead, they talked about the weather and crops. He felt ashamed that his own son was the one about to change their lives and he wanted to tell the King about how he felt, but he called his eldest daughter and she took them to a guest room and settled them in. He sent word that they will meet the next day, in the morning. They will then decide what to do about Finup.

Everybody was in the War Room, some sitting, some standing. The King was standing at the end of the long table discussing with Ropettian. On the table, in front of them, two wooden chests were open and their contents was laid on some tattered cloths. The King picked up a dagger and showing it to his companion pointed to the gems decorating its hilt.

"What do you think these stones represent, laid out like that?" he asked Ropé. The other man shrugged and looked around to find the scrolls he brought along. Maybe they could solve the mystery. Maybe together they will be able to conjure the spell or at least to understand the riddles. They have been trying without success to solve them and his frustration was growing.

Gumpen was sitting down, his cane resting on the side of this chair. He looked around and smiled sadly: his son should have been there too, only they were all there *because* of him, to try and persuade him to stop this madness. The windows were open and a cold breeze was blowing the curtains and that made him think of home. The crops were in the barns, the fields were plowed and everybody in Nill was getting ready for winter. Not many people knew about the war and the invasion. The Elders did, but they did not want to get the people worried yet. They were waiting for their King's orders. They did not come, but soon King Lade will send messengers far and wide to let everybody know about the imminent danger and that the men had to find their weapons and armours and get ready to go to war. A lot of families will be destroyed by this war and many people will join the Ancestors too soon.

As he was watching lost in thought, two white doves landed on the window sill and started cooing. Ropé looked at them surprised and moved closer to them. The birds did not seem scared of the people. They flew in and landed on the table. The flutter of their wings scattered the papers and some jumped up, scared by the unexpected appearance.

"Where have you been, my dears?" Ropé asked. He tried to catch one of the birds, but it flew away and landed on the back of one of the empty chairs. The other joined it and they both sat there looking around.

"These are the doves that guided us from our land to the city of Mortoria, a long time ago," Ropé continued. "They disappeared, only to show up again a few months before we left the city to come to Bridd." He moved closer, talking to the birds.

"I am not going to hurt you, I am glad you're back." He then turned to King Lade. "My Lord, we need to give them something to eat. For some reason they do not want to drink, but they would eat bread crumbs."

He looked around on the table and took some bread from one of the plates and started breaking it in small pieces. He threw the pieces on the floor and the birds jumped off the chairs and started pecking at them. Now everybody was standing up looking at the birds eat. To everybody's surprise, as soon as they finished, they jumped back on the chairs and seemed to rest like after a long trip.

"Let them rest and let's go back to our business," the King said to the others and as he was turning around, a warm breeze swept the room, scattering the papers again. A flash of light cracked and on the chairs where the birds have been sitting, two people appeared. The man was old, with gray hair and close cropped beard and the woman was young, beautiful, with long brown hair falling down her back.

The guards drew their swords and jumped in front of their master. The others backed up and grabbed their weapons pointing them at the two apparitions.

"Do not be frightened, my friends," the man spoke slowly and the King recognised the voice. It was the Spirit in the dungeons that had talked to him for the past few weeks.

"We come in peace. We are here to help you. Put your weapons down." The King pushed the guards gently to the side and moved close to the man.

"You are the Spirit in the library, are you not?" he asked excitedly. "Who are you? And why did you come now to us?"

The man stood up and his robes fluttered in an invisible breeze. He turned to his companion and they both looked fondly at the gathering.

"My name is Mortor and I was the leader of Mortoria. This is Johanna, the daughter of Torban. She is the one who warned us of General Gampill's coming and she tried to get the Ring back. She lost her life defending Mortoria and its people. She is the descendant of Nill Dorden, one of the twins who inherited the necklaces. It is her necklace that Marden sent to you, King Lade."

He stopped and smiled at the people in the room. Amazed, they did not know what to do, but after a few moments, Ropettian broke the awkward silence and moved closer to the woman. He tried to grab her hand, but he realised she was only a spirit and smiled.

"Welcome to our gathering, I assume you are here to help us defeat the Emperor?"

For the first time, Gumpen stood up and walked to the man who called himself Mortor.

"You knew my son, Finup, did you not? I am Gumpen, his father. He lived in Mortoria for some time, hasn't he?" He stopped and swallowed hard.

"I am sorry for all the death and destruction he caused. I thought I had raised him to be a good and kind man, but something happened and he changed into the evil man he is now. I . . ." Mortor interrupted the old man and smiled sadly at him.

"It is not your fault, Master Gumpen, Finup alone is responsible for his deeds. We need to find out how to stop him and we are here to help." He turned to the King.

"We are here to find out how to conjure the powers in these talismans. It may still work without the Ring, but we need to hurry. He is getting ready for the battle."

CHAPTER 21

The Foursome

"You need to bring the Book up here, King Lade. We need its wisdom to find out how to get the *Foursome* to work together." He saw the surprise on the man's face and continued.

"Now you are allowed to bring it here. Everybody in this room is a relative of King Bird. They all can learn now about the spell that protected these lands and they need to find out about their connection to the Ancestors."

The King stood up and left the room. Curious faces looked at him come back with a book with golden covers and spine. He put the heavy book on the table in front of him and looked at Mortor, waiting for him to give him instructions. But the Book knew what it had to do and opened once again. The King read: *The Foursome*. He had heard that name before and continued.

When the three brothers left their homeland with their gifts, the magic in them started fading. For the gifts to work their magic they had to be all together and they had to be held by their true owners. Should they fall into the wrong hands, their powers would still work, but only to subdue the evil. As soon as they came back to the Bird Kingdom, the power of the talisman would disappear and the thief would turn into the image of the Ancestors. They would not join them—the betrayal will prevent them from becoming spirits. They will be banned from their homeland and will not be able to return home for eternity.

The first son, Toran Bird inherited the Royal Dagger, being the first born and he passed it on to his first born, who passed it on to his first born. The last known descendant of King Toran Bird was King Rondal. He did not have any children of his own and his adoptive son, Nill, became the new ruler of the kingdom. It is then when the name of the kingdom changed to Bridd. The last known descendant of King Nill is Lade-Gleal.

The King stopped and a big sigh of relief echoed in the room as he continued with a shaky voice.

Toran Bird also inherited the Twin Necklaces, for him to give to his second and third born and if they would happen to be twins, their powers would be even stronger. In time, the necklaces became separated and King Bird's descendants passed them over to their own descendants. The last know owners of the necklaces are Johanna, daughter of Torban and Finup son of Gumpen. They were passed on by their great-grandparents Nill Larden and Ronda Norria, children of King Nill.

The King stopped again. The two necklaces were right here in the room but only one of the named descendants was. He looked at Gumpen who was staring at the necklace in shock and then at Johanna. The spirit of the young woman smiled back at him and gently touched the chain of the talisman she had given to Marden for safe keeping. Although she was a spirit, she could still lift it and the communion between the two shot blue sparks in the air. Everybody backed off but then realised the sparks were not real and laughter filled the room. The King resumed his reading once more.

The second son, Toran Mordon established the land of Mortoria and as he inherited the Sacred Ring, he passed it on to his descendants. It was thought to be lost, but many years ago it reappeared and the last known descendant of Toran Mordon is Mortor, the leader of Mortoria.

Without stopping, the King read on. *The third son, Toran Kostan inherited the Stone of Wisdom. He settled in the Land of Larmar where he lived until his time came to join the Ancestors. His last known descendant is Ropettian.*

The King stopped and took a deep breath. He knew all of this already, but what he didn't know was how to conjure the powers of the talismans. He looked at the spirit of Mortor and he pointed to the Book again. He looked at the pages and smiled.

Four generations ago, the Royal dagger was stolen by a distant cousin and then retrieved by King Sardan. The necklaces that were separated, lost most of their powers, the stone had been used only as an heirloom and the ring was locked in the vaults of Mortoria for safe keeping. The talismans are now scattered around the world and their powers are fading. They need to reunite one last time so their powers can be transferred back to their people. The Protector who knew how to conjure their powers had now passed, but he wrote it all in the scrolls that were passed on to King Toran. The riddles in the scrolls will help bring the powers back and the talismans will work together for the last time.

The King stopped again and looked worried to the gathering.

"There is nothing else written here. The Book ends. Whoever wrote this, did not know the spell or maybe did not want to reveal it for fear the Book could fall in the wrong hands. What are we going to do?"

Marden looked worried at his friend. They had to do something. He just returned from the meeting Finup had with the captains and the orders were clear: in the morning they were moving out to take over Bridd. With the Ring, he is powerful, but with the dagger, he would be invincible. Rotin stood up and looked outside to make sure nobody listened.

"We need to get the Ring, Marden. Without it, he is powerless. We can talk to some of the other captains and prepare to turn against him, but if he uses the Ring on us, he can kill everybody in the blink of an eye."

Marden looked at his friend.

"There may be a way to get the Ring back. Finup's man servant told me where he keeps it—apparently he is afraid someone would try to steal it and he keeps it in the General's tent, hidden in a small chest. We need to get it before a new day starts. We need a diversion."

Rotin added. "And we need to wait for night to fall. Do you trust this man? He is not trying to betray us?"

"No, he can be trusted, I knew his father. He is an honourable man, just like him," Marden said softly. "Let's get some rest. Tomorrow will be a long day."

The four men picked the talismans and put them in the middle of the table on the map of the land. This was their third try to conjure their powers; during the first two, nothing happened.

"Put the dagger on the City of Bridd, Gleal. Then, the necklaces should go on Nill and the other on Kunada. The stone on Larmar, and the ring on Mortoria. Let's see if anything happens." The King handed the pieces to his son and he placed them as he was told. They waited, but again nothing happened.

"Maybe we have to read the riddles as we do that," Ropé said. He looked around for the scrolls and gave one to each of the heirs.

"When I found the chest you had hidden in your front yard, Mortor, I tried to open it and it did not work. My daughters managed to open the box and when I read the riddle, a man appeared and told us that we need to get them all together to work. We are missing the Ring, but maybe we can still find out how to get them to work without it." He opened his scroll and gestured to the others to follow. Mortor added.

"I think you should start, King Gleal, the dagger was the first one to be mentioned in the Book. Then, the holders of the necklaces, Johanna and Gumpen. Next, I will read the riddle and last Ropé, since he has the stone."

The King took the dagger in his hand and read the riddle. Next came Johanna, then Gumpen, Mortor and Ropettian. They waited again and disappointed that nothing happened, they put the talismans on the table and sat down. The King was angry. The Book had guided him so far, Mortor had helped him understand what his role was and now none were able to tell them anything. He grabbed the Book and tried turning the pages angrily, surprised it let him do that.

"Why won't you tell us how to get the talismans to work? Why are the Ancestors angry at us?" he shouted. He dropped in his chair and looked at the others.

"Tomorrow we head out for Finup's camp and we have not been able to solve this mystery. If we cannot get the Ring back we are doomed." He stood up and grabbed his scroll and took another look at it. Desperate, he threw it on the table.

"We better get ready for tomorrow. Let's gather the talismans and the scrolls and put them in a safe place. Get some rest, we will start early in the morning."

As he turned to leave, he heard a voice and he stopped in his tracks. He knew that voice and looked up, hoping to see where it was coming from. But he couldn't see anybody and the others looked as shocked as him.

"Do you know who I am, King Lade-Geal?" The king nodded and answered with a shaky voice.

"Father, is that you? Are you here to help us?" The voice continued and everybody was now listening quietly. "I am here to tell you that you do not need to despair. You will defeat your enemy and help is waiting for you there, but you have to trust yourselves. You will be able to get the power of the *Foursome* to work again to save the people of Bridd and everybody else who was touched by Evil. Go ahead with your plan and believe in your faith. I will be watching you. Be safe!"

CHAPTER 22

The Final Battle

The horses were ready and the wagons loaded. The King was looking around at the soldiers and how serious they were going about their jobs. The rain was coming down hard and some of them were already soaked, but they did not care. They had a job to do and the bad weather would not stop them.

Gleal and Rehon were waiting in the saddles already, wrapped in the large cloaks. Gumpen was nestled inside one of the wagons and the driver was waiting for the order to move out. Mortor and Johanna had turned back into doves and were sitting on the canopy of Gumpen's wagon, flapping their wings to keep dry. They will join them too, maybe they could help contact Marden and Rotin.

Brohan arrived with Ropettian and joined the King. Their horses were saddled and they mounted. The others joined and lined up behind their captains. The King called to the men and everybody moved out. The women were left behind and tears were running down their faces. They did not know if they will see their loved ones again, but they knew the Ancestors will look after them.

The metal gates of the palace were wide open and the army moved out, horses in a quick trot and the wagons shaking and creaking. The streets were flanked by people waving and the women were throwing leaves at the soldiers. The last green leaves of the fall along with brown, dried ones covered the street and mixed with the rain were making the streets look like covered in blood.

A feeling of anxiety was filling their hearts, but they kept going. They had to stop Finup. They still didn't know how the talismans would work when they got close to the Ring, but they had to try to conjure their powers. The King wrapped himself in the cloak and pulled his helmet over his face to try and protect himself from the cold rain, but the water was still seeping through at the back. He shivered and looked at his companions. Their faces were covered by water and they were trying to wipe it off with the back of their hands, but it didn't help.

Suddenly he had a revelation: the united powers of the talismans had to somehow be related to them, all being together. Maybe if they *thought* about the riddles together and asked them for help! They hadn't tried this, and they did not have the Ring, but maybe being close to it would help. He called Ropettian who was riding beside him and the man pulled the horse closer.

"We have to try and take the Ring away from Finup. I think I know how to conjure the powers of the talismans. We may need the Ring, but it may work without it." The man nodded and slowed down his horse to talk to Gumpen.

"The King says that we have to get the Ring back from your son, but we may be able to conjure the powers of the other talismans without it." The old man shook his head. Who knows, maybe being close to him, could work. If they could not get it back, they had to try something else.

It was late in the evening and the rapping of the rain on the tent woke him up. He felt cold although he was wrapped in furs and blankets. The fire in the middle of the tent was burning and the crackling of the wood logs reminded him of home. Melancholy got to him all of a sudden and he could not shake it. That made him angry and throwing the covers down, called for his servant. The man came in bowing, bringing his meal and waited in a corner for him to finish. As soon as he was finished, he grabbed the plates, cleaned the small table and moved to the side.

"Is the General here?" he asked and the younger man shook his head. "Then go and fetch him," he barked at the frightened man who darted out of the tent. After a few moments, the flap door opened and the General came in. He bowed too, humbly and waited for his Master to talk.

"Are the captains ready? Are the horses ready? We need to move out in the morning." Then he stopped suddenly and turned around looking for something. "Where is the chest?" he shouted. He started to look through the covers, throwing them around.

"What are you looking for My Lord?" asked the General frightened.

"THE CHEST!" he bellowed. "The chest with the Ring and my dagger. Where is it?" He turned and looked for his servant, but he had already left. The General looked around, but he did not know what to look for and for a second thought of asking him, but then realised it was not a good time to ask such a question and opened the flap, calling for the servant.

The man showed up instantly, like he had been waiting outside and with frightened looks entered the tent.

"Where is the chest, Dorbin. It was here last night, what have you done with it?" The man looked at his master and answered with a shaky voice.

"You gave it to me to put it in the General's tent, for safe keeping. Like you have been doing it for some time now," he dared add and flinched, waiting for Finup to hit him. "I'll go get it." He turned and returned with a wooden box. Finup grabbed it and opened it with shaking hands. *It was there*, he let out a sigh of relief. It was there, safe and he took it and put it on. The Ring's powers seeped through this body and he felt empowered by it. Shaken by all of that, the General looked at him and turned to leave. Finup called him back.

"Get everybody ready, we are leaving in the morning. Bring Marden and Rotin over." He turned around and sat down in his throne. The servant picked up the furs and wrapped him up.

Quietly he left the tent. *Maybe I can have a quick word with Captain Marden before they settled down for the night. I need to tell him about the Ring. Maybe he can take it and stop this madness. I will make my father proud, if I could only resist a little while longer. After all this suffering, I will make sure the Ring went back to its rightful owner. Mortoria and my father's death will be avenged.*

The young man covered himself in the thin cape and entered a small tent to the side of the Emperor's. The rain was hitting it hard and the rapping reminded him of home. He knew it will never be like before but he hoped some day they will be able to return home and rebuild their lives.

Rotin pulled the flap to the tent and entered, lowering his head. Marden followed quietly and the men stopped in front of the throne.

"You called us, My Lord," Marden asked and Finup looked at them with a smirk on his face.

"We are getting ready to head for Bridd. Do you have anything you need to tell me, anything that I should know before we get there?"

The two men looked at each other and shrugged.

"No, My Lord, there is nothing else you need to know," Marden answered. "We will encounter some resistance but nothing to worry about. Like I said, the kingdom doesn't have a regular army, so even if we have to go to battle, it will end quickly. Once they are out of the way we can get to the palace and find the dagger. When you will have the Ring *and* the dagger you will be the most powerful man in this part of the world."

Finup pushed the furs down and moved closer to the two men.

"I hope you are right. My scouts returned and told me that the army does not look that unprepared. They have riders covered in armour and they carry something in large wagons. What do you think it could be in there?" He turned around and laughed defiantly.

"Whatever it is, there is nothing compared to what I have prepared for them. The Ring will be my most powerful weapon and I will use it as soon as we get close to them. You can watch how I will win this battle without shooting one arrow or firing one cannon. The power of the Ring will do all the work for me. Go now, I need to rest. I will see you in the morning."

He dismissed them and as they were exiting the tent, they could hear him cackle. Disgusted, they headed back to their tents, but a young man peeked from a small tent and called them.

"Captain Marden, Master Rotin, I need to talk to you, it is a matter of life and death." The two men looked at each other and entered the tent looking around to make sure nobody saw them.

The King raised his hand and the men stopped. His companions pulled their horses closer and they all dismounted. Gumpen joined them, coming out of the wagon. He was wrapped in blankets and looked alert, but they could tell that the cold weather has started to get to him. The Chief of the Guards came running and the King turned to him.

"We can stop here for the night, Gardall. Have the men put up the tents and start up the fires. We need to warm up. Gleal, Rehon, help the men with the horses and then join us for the evening meal. Myrdall, set up the night watches, we need to be on the lookout in case the Emperor wants to surprise us."

He looked at the sky. The rain had stopped, but the ground was soggy and he knew it will be a cold night. He thought about the loved ones they have left behind and hoped they will see each other again. Tomorrow they will get ready for the battle and he hoped the outcome would be in their favour. Brohan joined him and the two men walked together toward the fire the men had started. The water was boiling and the food was cooking. It will be a long night, but they were together now and with their united forces will get rid of the evil.

The rain had stopped and the young man sneaked out of the camp. He was trying to use the moon's light to find his way around the tents and wagons. Horses were nodding covered by big blankets and he used them to hide from the soldiers. The guards were patrolling up and down the paths between the rows of tents and he waited for them to move away before he continued on his way. Finally he reached the edge of the camp and crouching down he looked behind him. Nobody followed, he was safe. He started running and soon he was at a safe distance from the camp so he stopped, panting. He could see the Bridd army's camp in the distance—the fires were showing him the way. He started running again and soon he saw the first guards. He did not want to risk being killed by mistake, so he stood up and called to the men. One of the soldiers turned suddenly and raised his crossbow.

"Don't shoot!" he called desperately. "I need to talk to your Master. I come from the Emperor's camp and I have important information." He stopped and allowed the other man to come closer. He raised his arms and started walking slowly toward him. The soldier called out to another man, not letting his eyes off the stranger and he came running with his sword drawn.

"Who are you and what are you doing here at this time of night?" he asked. "Go and wake up Young Master Gleal. We caught a spy," he said to the other man.

"I'm not a spy! Please, you have to believe me. I come with news from Captain Marden. I know where the Ring is."

Gleal showed up running and when he heard the man talking about the ring he stopped in his tracks.

"Bring him to me, I will take him to my father. Wake him and Master Ropettian up. Tell them that a messenger from Marden is here. Hurry!" He told the guard to escort the stranger and they all moved to the central tent. He wondered what the man knew about the Ring and if he was really a messenger and not a spy.

It was the middle of the night and the King's tent was lit by torches and people were coming and going. In its middle, a campfire was crackling and from time to time, Rehon would throw a piece of wood in it to keep it going. The King, Ropé, Brohan and Gumpen were all sitting around the fire. Mortor had changed back to his own self and they were all waiting for young Gleal to come and join them. He finally showed up and held the flap open. The guard pushed someone inside and Mortor gasped.

"Dorbin? What are you doing here, son? Where are you mother and sister?" The man stopped suddenly and looked at the translucent silhouette.

"Father, is it really you?" Then he realised he looked different and asked with a shaking voice. "What happened to you?"

Gleal turned to Mortor and asked him. "Do you know this man? He says he comes from the Emperor's camp and knows where the Ring is." Mortor turned to the men who were looking at him intrigued and said.

"This is my son, Dorbin. I thought he left Mortoria with the others, but I see now that he did not follow my orders."

He turned back to the young man and asked him again.

"Where is your sister? What are you doing in Finup's army? Did he take you prisoner and forced you to fight in his army?" Dorbin answered bitterly.

"No, father, I was taken prisoner but I did not fight in battle, I *served* him. I brought him food and water and washed him and clothed him. He humiliated me and he made me his servant. But at least Silvana is safe. She managed to escape and is now in the land of Kunada with Mother and the rest of the family."

There was anger in his voice, but he stopped and pulled himself together.

"But that is not why I am here. I know where the Emperor keeps the Ring and I told Captain Marden and Master Rotin. They will try to take it tonight and keep it safe." As they all looked surprised, he continued.

"I know about the powers of the Ring, Master Marden told me about it some time ago. He saw me once when I was serving *him* and sent for me. He recognised me and explained that we needed to convince him to keep the Ring away from him, in case someone would try to steal it. So he came with the idea of putting it in a chest, but we didn't know where he kept it. I found out a few days ago when he sent me to take it to the General's tent. I don't know why he sent me, usually he would look after that, but maybe because he is more confident now." He looked at his father and smiled.

"I hope you are proud of me, Father. I endured humiliation and beatings, but I knew that would not be in vain. I knew the time would come when I could help defeat the evil and *now* it is the time. I talked with Captain Marden before coming here and he said they will try to get the Ring from Gumpen's tent and hide it, but they knew they could not hold on to it for too long."

The moon was high in the sky and the men moved quietly between the tents. They had to get into the General's tent and find the box, but they didn't know how they will be able to do that. They could go in and ask the General to give the box to them, but he has been very suspicious lately and he could go to Finup and ask for confirmation. They had to find another way. Then, they saw the campfire throwing shadows around and they looked at each other, smiling wickedly. Marden grabbed a piece of burning wood and lit one corner of the tent. The fabric was still damp, but it finally caught fire and the two put the burning wood down, hid behind a wagon and waited.

Soon, one of the soldiers noticed the fire and shouted at a group sleeping on the ground, wrapped in furs. They all grabbed some buckets and started throwing water on the tent, but it continued burning. They went inside to get the General out and soon he appeared half naked with a bewildered look on his face. He started bellowing at the soldiers, who were frantically trying to put out the fire, but they did not have enough water and some grabbed some blankets and tried to smother it with them.

The two men looked at each other again and waited until only a couple of soldiers were around and pretended to help. They grabbed some blankets and entered the tent telling the soldiers to wake up more people to help put out the fire. They were inside, without anybody wondering what they were doing there and started looking around. They saw the General's cot and turned it upside down. Smiling, they picked the chest up and rushed out of the burning tent. Hardly anything was left of one side, so they had to hurry, they did not want to get buried in the tarp that was about to come down.

Soon, nothing was left of the tent and the tired soldiers stopped. The fire finally went out by itself and they were just standing there, looking at the ashes, ambers flying around in the cold breeze. The General showed, followed by Finup who, at the sight of the burned down tent, started wailing. He pushed away one of the soldiers closest to him, ordering him to go and look for the chest, but he refused. The General grabbed a sword from one of the soldiers standing around and started searching the debris. He did not find anything and turned to his Master.

"It is gone, My Lord, it was destroyed in the fire. Forgive me, my Master. I don't know how that was possible."

Mad with desperation, Finup grabbed the sword from Gampill's hand and hit him with all his might.

"YOU ARE RESPONSIBLE FOR THIS!" he bellowed. You will pay for your incredible stupidity." He leaned over the frightened man, lying on the ground.

"You will pay with your life for what you have done," he barked. A nonhuman scream filled the night air and the horses neighed frightened. Finup felt powerless and fell on his knees, sobbing. For the first time in his life he wished he was dead.

The commotion in the enemy's camp could be heard across the field and a bright light coming from somewhere in its centre could be seen from the King's camp. Some soldiers woke up and stood up looking in the other camp's direction. They pointed to the growing light and more joined them. The guards around the King's tent were turning to see what the noise was about and they too, saw the light. One of them entered the tent and told the people inside that something was happening in the enemy camp and everybody came out. The light grew even bigger in the sky and they realised it was a fire burning out of control.

Dorbin smiled and told the King.

"This must be Captain Marden, trying to get the Ring. That is the General's tent that is burning." He laughed and turned to the others.

"He managed to take the Ring, My Lord. He's done it. I just know it!" Mortor came close to his son and although he knew he could not hug him, he put his arm around him. The young man felt a warm breeze surrounding him and smiled. Then he fell on his knees and looked at the night sky.

"I knew the Ancestors would look after us. I knew my suffering would not be in vain. Thank you," he said softly.

The first to come out of shock was Brohan. He moved closer and grabbed him, standing him on his feet.

"Master Dorbin, we need to get the Ring. How can we find Marden and Rotin?" Mortor stepped forward.

"*I* will go get it. I can fly there without anyone seeing me and I know them. They will trust me—they were there when I joined the Ancestors. It is thanks to them that we are here now," he said turning to Johanna who has been standing quietly behind them, "and not rotting in a field without a tomb." As he was flying toward to the camp, a cry rose in the air. It filled everybody with a feeling of despair and they knew something bad had happened.

It was morning and the King was in his tent. Nobody had slept last night. They all waited for Mortor to come back with the Ring. The time has passed very slowly but finally they heard wings flutter and they knew he was back. The soldiers brought torches and held them high to light the area. Tied to one of his legs, there it was! Mortor landed on the canopy of a wagon nearby and Dorbin grabbed him gently. He untied the ring off his leg and handed it to the King. He did not touch it, though. He smiled and pushed his hand back.

"It is yours, you are the rightful owner of the Ring." Mortor had returned to his human shape now and nodded.

"Yes, my son, after my passing you would have gotten it, you are my first born. The talismans are meant to move on to the next generation. You are Mortoria's next generation. You look after our people and lead them with kindness and wisdom." The young man looked around proudly and put the Ring on his finger. Its power surged in his body and he felt stronger than ever. The magic in its stone has found its rightful heir. They were one now.

It was time now to get the talismans together. They have been reunited and their rightful owners where here. Their combined powers should stop Finup and they all got together around the fire. In front of the King's tent, the soldiers made a half circle around it, waiting quietly. The King came out and a murmur rose from the crowd.

"It is time, my friends," he started. "It is time to see the power of the people of Bridd at work. We have the *Foursome* and we need to conjure their powers to stop the battle."

He turned to Ropettian and asked him to come forward.

"Bring the Stone of Wisdom, heir of Toran Kostan." The man moved forward and took the stone out of his pocket. He then turned to Gumpen.

"Bring the first of the necklaces, heir of King Nill," he called again. Gumpen stepped forward slowly, leaning on his cane. He took the necklace from around his neck and held it in his hand.

"Bring the Sacred Ring, heir of King Mordon," he called to Dorbin and the young man stepped closer to the others and took the Ring off his finger. Last, he turned to Johanna and smiling he gave her the second necklace.

"Come forward, daughter of Torban and second heir of King Nill." She took the necklace and it shone brightly. The young woman shivered as she touched it and joined the others. Then the King took the dagger out of his pocket and held it up high.

"Here I stand, the true heir of King Bird and I bring forward the Royal Dagger."

Cheers rose from the crowd, filling the cold morning air. The five people held their talismans up in their hands, in a circle. For a moment, nothing happened, but then their hands started shaking and they could not hold on to their gifts. Sparks started shooting out of the dagger and the stone started to glow brightly. The necklaces rose in the air and merged into one. Last, the ring's gem turned to a bright red and the rays connected. Magical sparks surrounded the hands of the five people. Under the joined hands, a blue flame appeared suddenly and everybody looked at it worried, but the flame was cold.

The power of the *Foursome* grabbed the five people and lifted them gently in the air keeping them there for a few moments. Then, slowly, they floated back on the ground and the talismans returned to their owners. The glowing stopped and the fire put itself out. The necklaces separated and the ring's gem turned back to its original purple colour. Everybody sighed and looked around to see if anything had changed, when a wave of light, followed by a loud boom shot outwards, surrounding the men in the camp and went as far as the Emperor's camp. Then silence filled the air. A feeling of relief filled everybody's hearts and the crowd erupted in cheers. The magic of the *Foursome* had worked.

There was no movement in the Emperor's camp. Nobody could be seen on the paths, or around the campfires. The silence was eerie and when Marden came out of his tent he looked around to see what was going on. He walked over to Rotin's tent and as he came out, he too, looked surprised.

"Where is everybody?" he asked and the other man shrugged. They headed for Finup's tent, entering and being surprised that nobody stopped them. They finally opened the flap to the main room and saw him. He was half turned away from them, but they could tell it was him.

"Are you all right, My Lord?" Rotin started, but as the man turned he stopped, shocked. "What happened to you? What have you become?" he asked again. The creature opened his mouth to answer but instead a honking sound came out. He tried again, but the same strange sound came out. Sadly, he turned around and sat down on the ground.

The two men looked at each other and suddenly started laughing. Roaring, they looked at what was left of Finup and tried to talk, but they chocked and laughed some more. After a while they stopped, tears running down their cheeks and looked at what was left of their former master.

"The Ancestors have punished you for trying to take what was not yours, Finup. You turned against your people and family and you got what you deserved. You brought this onto yourself and nobody can help you now." They turned around and left the tent. Rotin stopped in the doorway and smiling, added.

"Now we are free to go home and start our new lives. Thank the Ancestors for looking after us. A new life begins." A cackle came from the tent and they knew it was Finup who was sobbing.

It was finally over!

EPILOGUE

The wedding bells were ringing and the bride and groom came out of the palace. The young woman was smiling and was holding her new husband's hand. The groom was walking slowly looking at the crowd cheering outside the palace's gates. The women had been throwing flowers and the steps were covered by them. The newlyweds walked down the steps and stopped to wave at the people who joined in their happiness. The King followed them shortly with Brohan and his wife. The woman was smiling, tears in her eyes. The other guests started to come out of the palace and they all stopped in front of the gate.

King Lade shook the groom's hand and hugged the bride.

"Be happy, my daughter and may the Ancestors watch over you two." He then turned to the groom. "You keep her safe and happy. You have my blessings, Myrdall. May the Ancestors watch over you!" he said again. The crowd cheered again and the young woman blushed. He grabbed her husband's hand and the two headed for the carriage waiting for them.

"Farewell, Father and be safe! Come and visit us soon." She smiled at him and the old man kissed her on the cheek.

"Farewell, Llewella, I will come to visit as soon as your brother is ready to take over the reins of the kingdom." He turned to Gleal and looked fondly at him.

"You are ready to become the next King, my son. The Ancestors told me so." The young man looked surprised at his father and nodded.

"Me too, Father. I have known it for some time. I am glad you trust me. Mother would be so proud of me." He then turned to his sister.

"Happy travels, my sister, Myrdall is very fortunate to have you. Come and visit us in the big city." The young woman hugged him and kissed him on the cheek, then stepped in the carriage. Myrdall joined her and the driver turned to him.

"Let's go! Let's take my bride to our new home. May the Ancestors watch over you, Father and Mother," he shouted over to his parents. His voice got lost in the cheers as they waved goodbye. The driver called to the horses and the carriage moved away slowly. The King smiled and looked at the sky. He knew his wife would be watching and he knew he would soon join her. But there were a few more things to do before that and they all went back in the palace. Young Gleal was ready to take over and he was ready to pass the burden over to him.

"Grandpa, what happened to the evil emperor?" a sweet voice asked the old man sitting in the rocking chair by the fireplace. The man looked at the little girl and smiled.

"He was banished to a cold and deserted land for what he had done, my sweet. He was never allowed to join the Ancestors and his soul wanders around without finding peace."

"But what did he turn into, Grandfather," the serious voice of a young boy asked.

"Into a small, black bird with short legs that likes the cold lands of the Everlasting Ice. It is called a puffin."

"And is it then when the prophecy said that all Bridd people would turn to birds when they joined the Ancestors?" This time it was the voice of a young woman who asked the question. The old man turned and looked at her smiling.

"You very well know that the prophecy did not say that, young lady! It was the spirit of King Bird that showed after the magic was conjured, who said that from then on all people will turn to birds upon their passing on to the spirits."

He smiled fondly at her and she hugged him, kissing him on the cheek.

"Are you making up stories again, Father?" Then she turned to the children huddled around him.

"It's bed time, you little ones. Off you go, it's late." The children let out disappointed groans, but stood up and kissed their grandfather good night. The older boy turned around and in a very serious voice told the old man.

"You still have to tell us what happened to great-grandfather Ropettian and old man Gumpen and the late King Lade-Gleal, grandfather." As he was going to bed, he turned like he had forgotten something.

"And if the protective spell was broken, too, Grandpa."

"Another time, son, this is a story for another time. Now you listen to your mother and go to bed. Good night!" He stood up and grabbed his daughter's arm.

"Let's take you to bed too, Master Frotin. I am sure Mother is waiting for you." The old man stopped and looked at his daughter. She looked so much like his wife. Only Solanna had green eyes and her hair used to be chestnut brown. Her daughter had black eyes and dark hair, just like him. She was the perfect combination of wisdom and kindness. Just like her grandfather, Ropettian would have liked to see.

If you liked my book please go to http://mdmillar.com and leave a comment in my blog.
Thank you!
M. D. Millar

GLOSSARY OF CHARACTERS

King Lade-Gleal—son of King Sardan, had five children, three sons and two daughters. The eldest son, Gleal is also his heir. He led the army to defeat Finup (The Emperor). He inherited the Royal Dagger—which had been stolen by a distant relative, but retrieved by his father—and one of the Twin Necklaces. Upon his passing, according to the prophecy, he turned into a bald eagle, the king of birds.

Finup—Son of Gumpen. He is the last known descendant of King Nill's only daughter, Ronda Norria. He left Nill to go to the capital city and eventually left Bridd. He wandered around the world and finally arrived in Mortoria, where became a Councillor. He stole the Sacred Ring from Mortor and with its powers took over General Gumpill's army. On the way to take over Bridd, he lost the Ring and the power of the *Foursome* turned him into a puffin. He was exiled to the Land of Everlasting Ice.

Ropettian (Ropé)—Leader of the group of people who left Larmar to find their brothers and sisters and join in the battle against Finup. He married Traciana and had two twin daughters. He inherited the Stone of Wisdom from his father, who got it by marrying one of the descendants of Toran Kostan. He was the last known descendant of King Nill's youngest son, Nill Larden.

Mortor—Leader of the City of Mortoria, he welcomed Finup in his city and helped him settle in. He had inherited the Sacred Ring and kept it in the City Hall vault. Mortor is killed by Finup because he would not give up the secret of the Ring. He turned into the spirit that helped King Lade find and understand the *Book of Wisdom*.

Dorbin—Mortor's son. Is captured by Finup and turned into his servant. Dorbin escaped on the eve of the battle and told King Lade about the Ring and how Marden and Rotin would try to take it away from Finup. He was the heir of Mortoria and the last holder of the Ring.

Marden and **Rotin**—Friends of Finup, they left together from their village and went to the capital city. They joined Finup in his travels and ended up in Mortoria, where they settled. When Finup stole the Ring, the two joined his army to try to get the Ring back. They buried Mortor and Johanna to help them pass on. Marden sends a messenger to King Lade with the other twin necklace and to warn him of the danger Finup poses. They managed to get the Ring back and returned it to Dorbin.

Young Prince Gleal—The heir of King Lade and his eldest son. He goes to Nill to bring Gumpen, Finup's father to the capital city, to help defeat his son.

Johanna—Daughter of Torban, she traveled to Mortoria to warn Mortor about the dangers of General Gampill's army. She helped defend the city, but died of her injuries after being tortured by Finup to give up the secret of the Ring. She turned into a spirit and joined Mortor. Together they guided Ropé's party to Mortoria and helped conjure the power of the *Foursome*.

General Gampill—Started a long and cruel campaign of war and destruction, taking over land after land. His cruelty was renowned in his native land of Parmonish. He met Finup and made an alliance with him to conquer Mortoria, but Finup took him under control with the help of the Ring. He was killed by Finup on the battle field and turned into a magpie, cursed to look for shiny things for eternity.

Gumpen—Finup's father and the direct descendant of Ronda Norria, King Nill's daughter. He gave Finup one of the twin necklaces and he was the reason Finup fled Nill. He went to the capital city to help the King defeat his own son and helped conjure the power of the *Foursome*. Upon his passing, he turned into a penguin and lives in the Land of Everlasting Ice, looking for his son.

Brohan—First Councillor to King Lade. He left the capital city to meet Ropettian and reunite them with their kin. He helped the King prepare for the battle. His son Myrdall, married the King's eldest daughter, Llewella.

Ronden and **Khiran**—Former soldiers in the palace's guards. Were sent to retrieve the dagger from a vault and went to the King to let him know about the presence of the dagger in the dungeons.

AUTHOR'S BIOGRAPHY

M. D. Millar, pen name for Maria Dumitrescu, was born in Bucharest, Romania. Her writing career started in school when she placed 3rd in an interschool competition of compositions for Mother's Day in her hometown. While in university, she wrote a number of articles for the Romanian Academy of Sciences Annuals and after graduation she published a series of newspaper articles in a Medical Journal. In 2008, she coordinated and developed a resource manual for ESL and literacy instructors, currently available online.

Graduate of the University of Bucharest and holding a B.A. and an M.A. in languages and linguistics she always dreamt of writing children and youth books.

The Secret of Bridd is her first fictional youth novel about loyalty and sacrifice. The characters in the story fight, and die, to protect the most important things in our lives: family and friends. Not always Good defeats Evil, but when all the *good guys* join together in the fight, Evil has no choice but to retreat and surrender.

M. D. currently lives in Calgary, Alberta, Canada with her son and husband.

CPSIA information can be obtained at www.ICGtesting.com
Printed in the USA
LVOW12s1031240813

349392LV00006B/18/P